Semi-Sane
Harper Hall Investigations #5

Isabel Jordan

Copyright © 2017 Isabel Jordan

All rights reserved.

ISBN-10: 1979536252
ISBN-13: 978-1979536257

Praise for *Semi-Charmed*

"Harper is a heroine you can get behind! She's witty, crazy, kick-ass, and amazing! Noah is my new book boyfriend! He's the bad boy we all want and your mom hates but then she falls in love with him, too!"

—Indy Book Fairy

"Fresh and fun. Relaxed with a good dose of humor."
—Lanie's Book Thoughts

"Semi-Charmed is well-paced, fun and easy to read."
—TJ Loves to Read

"The hero and heroine were intriguing and engaging."
—Smexy Books

"Holy crap! That was awesome! More please!! Brilliantly funny, sexy, charming, and awesome."
Me, Myself & Books

"If you are a fan of the Sookie Stackhouse books, Buffy the Vampire slayer, and the likes, you will enjoy this book a great deal."
—The Book Disciple

Praise for *Semi-Human*

"A fun and sexy, sweet and exciting story about a smart, witty and kick-ass heroine, a swoony, intense and equally badass hero." --TJ Loves to Read

"Harper Hall is the best kind of heroine for me. She's funny, snarky, can handle herself in a fight and never shies away from telling anyone what she's thinking. Long-story-short, this series is worth a read. Just don't read it in public because there are parts that are snort-laugh inducing (and no one looks hot while snort-laughing)." --Knockin' Books

"As for Riddick, well that dude just has issues. I'm just gonna say it, he's that really hot guy, ya know the one who's crazy that you should inch away from, but instead you give your number. Yep, that one." --Lanie's Book Thoughts

"The snark, the humor, the sarcasm, the love. This is a well-rounded, well-written novel and an awesome progression for the series." --Me, Myself & Books

"I went into this book hoping to get the same feelings I got from the last book. I was not disappointed. This book was great from beginning to end. The characters I loved in the last book were there for me again." --Pixies Can Read Blogspot

Praise for *Semi-Twisted*

"Isabel Jordan delivers a laugh out loud, action packed, entertaining read with sassy dialogues and pop culture references that made me smile like a loon." --TJ Loves to Read

"All in all, as with other books in the series, this one is perfect for fans of the PNR genre, and for fans of adult contemporary romance with lots of humor and just a hint of edge. It's definitely one for the keeper shelves!" --Knockin' Books

"If you love Charley Davison, True Blood or Buffy the Vampire Slayer, then you will definitely want to read this quirky vampire/paranormal series." –Literati Literature Lovers

"I waited FOREVER for this book…at least it seemed that way. I couldn't wait to read Mischa and Hunter's story! True to the author's form, I giggled my way through this story, when I wasn't sighing over the leading man." –Author L.E. Wilson

Praise for *Semi-Broken*

"Shifters and dhampyres, wit, humor and excitement, acceptance and love. Isabel Jordan delivers it all in Semi-Broken, another wonderful installment in the Harper Hall Investigations series." –TJ Loves to Read

"This book and series has quickly become a comfort series to me. When I need a good read with some quirky but lovable characters this is definitely on the list! There is plenty of snark, sarcasm, wit, and friendly banter that happens between these characters that I just connect to them all. I just can't get enough!" –The Genre Minx

"It reads like a perfect blend of all my favorite romantic comedies, action movies and supernatural TV shows." –Romance Rehab

DEDICATION

To all the ladies in my *Bitch, Write Faster* group. Without your support (and constant nagging), this book never would've been finished. I can't thank you all enough!

ACKNOWLEDGMENTS

First of all, thanks to my son, Connor, for your unwavering faith and support. I hope to one day be as famous as you seem to think I already am.

Thanks to my husband, Don. I really do appreciate all the times you let me rage and vent about how badly my fictional characters were misbehaving, and never let me feel like I'm *too* crazy because of it.

Thanks to my parents for their continued support. I hope to one day be as talented and awesome as you seem to think I already am.

Thanks to The Design Dude at Romance Rehab for another awesome cover. Despite your misgivings, I think you did a lovely job with Meth Girl and Mr. Magoo.

HUGE thanks to Renee Wright for your eagle proofreading and editing eye yet again. (Sorry for all the emdash and hyphen errors. I'm sure I'll understand how to properly use them someday.)

Thanks to LE Wilson, beta reader extraordinaire. Once again, this book never would have made it out of the draft phase if not for you being there to prop my ego and confidence up whenever necessary.

And last by certainly not least, thank you to all the wonderful readers out there who have stuck with Harper and her crew for the duration of the series. Your support means more to me than you could ever know—more than I could ever express (which is saying a lot, because I'm SUPER wordy). Thanks is still totally inadequate, but, yeah, there it is…

Chapter One

As it turned out, Stockholm syndrome didn't go away immediately after a daring rescue. Nope. Apparently, it could jump up and smack a victim in the face months later. Four months, three days, eight hours, and a handful of minutes, to be exact.

Not that she was counting.

Dr. Violet Marchand was somewhat of an expert on all things Stockholm syndrome for a couple of reasons. Number one, she was a psychiatrist. A damn good one, too. She even had the fancy diploma from Johns Hopkins to prove it. Not to mention she was one of the only therapists in the state of New York to earn a license to treat supernatural patients.

But that was a different story entirely.

The point was that she now had irrefutable, empirical evidence of the impact of Stockholm syndrome on the human body. Her body, specifically. Or, even more specifically, her nipples.

Because at that very moment, she stood in the doorway of her apartment, face to face—or, face to chest, she supposed, because he was *really* tall—with the man who'd taught her more about Stockholm syndrome than textbooks and years of clinical practice ever could.

Nikolai Aleyev, the man who'd stalked her, fake-dated her, drugged her, and kidnapped her, all to get close to one of her patients—who he intended to kill—was here in front of her. And after everything he'd done to her, her nipples were on high alert, practically saluting the man like a lowly private salutes a four-star general at West Point. Stockholm syndrome in action.

Stupid traitorous nipples.

Violet held up her phone, with one finger poised over the screen to call for help. "One wrong move and I hit this button, which will automatically call 911."

The bastard had the nerve to smile at her as he held up his hands in supplication. "I mean you no harm, *kotehok*."

Kotehok. Russian for kitten. She brutally tamped down the obnoxious, fluttery…Stockholm syndrome-y feelings the nickname set off in her stomach. She refused—absolutely *refused*—to fall for cutesy nicknames and that low, growly, sexy Russian accent of his.

Well, *again*, anyway.

And besides, she only had his word for it that *kotehok* meant kitten, anyway. She didn't speak Russian. For all she knew, he was really calling her a simple-minded chump in that sexy accent.

Violet lowered the phone but kept it in her hand, just in case. "Who let you in the building, Nikolai?"

He leaned a shoulder against her doorjamb, not looking at all concerned that she had a twitchy 911 finger. "Small woman." He held a hand up to indicate the woman in question had been about armpit height on him. "About sixty years old. Asked me if I was single. Wouldn't let me in until I said yes."

Violet suppressed a groan. Mrs. Copely. The woman was desperately looking for a man to marry her daughter and give her grandbabies. She would've let Ted Bundy into the building if she thought his sperm count was high enough.

And Nikolai Aleyev looked like every woman's *dream* sperm donor.

Tall, dark, and dangerous, with chiseled bone structure, messy hair the color of melted dark chocolate, dark brows slashing over pale green eyes, a flawless olive complexion lily-white people like Violet would *kill* for…yep. The sperm bank—or Mrs. Copely's daughter, for that matter—would probably *kill* to take a dip in Nikolai's gene pool.

"What do you want?" she asked, ruthlessly dragging her attention away from thoughts of Nikolai's presumably grade-A swimmers.

"I only want a few minutes of your time. Then I'll leave you alone." He glanced at the phone in her hand. "You don't need that. I won't hurt you."

"Again," she said quietly. "You won't hurt me *again*."

He winced, but held her gaze. "No. Never again."

They both knew she wasn't talking about hurt in the physical sense, either. He was too diabolical for that. During the whole kidnapping ordeal he'd been nothing but gentle with her. Tender, even. No, her scars from that night weren't physical.

Emotional dings and bruises were another matter entirely.

There'd been a time with him, right before the kidnapping, when she'd been sure he was *The One*. She'd let her natural defenses down with him in ways she never had before. He'd seen more of her—the real her, not the serious, professional mask she usually let the world see—than anyone she'd ever known. She'd been within kissing distance of falling for him.

And damned if that thought didn't remind her of the one and only kiss they'd shared. A kiss she'd initiated, of course—the best of her life. Which only deepened her humiliation where this man was concerned.

How utterly clueless and naïve she'd been to think he'd felt *any* of what she was feeling.

Violet stared at him for what felt like an eternity, searching for something, *anything*, that would tell her he was lying to her now. That he had some kind of new agenda. She found nothing. He sounded and looked totally sincere.

And that just pissed her off. Hating him would be *so* much easier if he was a lying bastard, incapable of empathy or love or any other messy human emotion.

She cleared her throat. "Talk fast. I have to get ready for work."

If he was at all put off by her abrupt tone, his stoic facial expression certainly gave no indication. "I have a job in town, so I'll be here in Whispering Hope at least for a few months. I wanted you to know so that if you saw me somewhere, you wouldn't be caught unaware."

Unaware? You mean, like I am now, as I stand here with nothing but a thin robe covering my flannel pajama pants with little light sabers all over them and the tank top with Yoda's face and the words "There Is No Try" printed across my boobs?

She was about to inform him that the best way to avoid catching someone unaware was to *call them* before you showed up on their doorstep when a disturbing thought occurred to her. "What kind of job?" she asked, her tone ripe with suspicion. "You're not—"

One dark brow rose. "Here to kill someone?" he finished her sentence for her in a tone drier than Death Valley sand. "No, Violet. The Council helped me get a construction job with a company downtown."

She took a relieved breath, even though she logically knew the vampire Council wouldn't let him pick up his life where Sentry left off. They wouldn't have let him ever see the light of day again if they thought he was a danger to anyone.

He tipped his head down so he could look her straight in the eye and quietly said, "I'm not crazy, *kotehok*. I know what I did to you was wrong. I just didn't know what else to do at the time."

Violet wanted to ignore the stab of sympathy she felt for him. She *really* wanted to. But she just couldn't. She knew too much about ex-Sentry employees—and about Nikolai specifically— not to sympathize with him, no matter what he'd done to her.

Back before vampires came out of the coffin, paranormal threats against human society were policed by Sentry, an organization with endlessly deep pockets and ties to every government in the world. Such threats were eliminated without prejudice.

All that ended when the vampires peeled back the curtain on their society, exposing Sentry in the process. The organization didn't fare too well in the court of public opinion. The vampires had made sure of it.

When Sentry folded, thousands of people were out of work. People who'd been told they were heroes, helping to safeguard humanity, were suddenly hated for no other reason than their association with Sentry. That kind of thing tended to scar even the most resilient psyches, which was where Vi came in.

Most of her ex-Sentry patients hated themselves for what they'd been forced to do for their organization more than anyone else ever could. Nikolai wasn't her patient, but she could easily see that he fell into that category.

Nikolai was a *dhampyre*, a genetically engineered vampire/human hybrid, and like her former patient, Seven, he'd been a cleaner for Sentry. As Seven had explained it to her, cleaners were essentially trained to kill anyone and anything that stood between them and whatever mission Sentry had assigned to them. If they resisted, they were sent for "reprogramming," which was basically just a euphemism for months of solitary confinement, brainwashing, and torture.

Since the time his parents were murdered and he was sold to Sentry when he was only five years old, Nikolai had been sent for reprogramming four times. As far as she knew, no one else had ever been sent for reprogramming more than once.

Cleaners set about killing each other when Sentry folded, as they'd been trained to do. As far as anyone knew, Nikolai and Seven were the last of their kind. Thank God Seven had been able to reason with Nikolai, or else they'd probably both be dead now.

But not before he'd kidnapped Violet to get to Seven.

Logically, Violet knew not to doubt the Council's judgment. They were all ancient vampires, with Hunter, her friend Mischa's husband, being the oldest of all. Combined, they had *thousands* of years' worth of wisdom under their belts. If they thought Nikolai wasn't a danger to society, he most likely wasn't.

But her not-so-logical heart still saw him for the predator he was. She wasn't about to usher Nikolai back into her life with open arms (or legs, for that matter).

That kind of hurt and humiliation just wasn't something she'd ever subject herself to again.

Mask of calm professionalism firmly back in place (even though her heart and stomach were warring for a spot in her throat), she said, "Thank you for telling me. Is that all?"

Something she couldn't quite identify flashed in his eyes. Pain? Maybe a little regret? She wasn't sure, and it was gone before she could make sense of it. "I also wanted to tell you that I'm sorry," he said.

Violet crossed her arms over her chest, steeling herself against the sincerity in his tone, the warmth in his eyes. "For what? For fake dating me? Kidnapping me? Trying to kill one of my patients?"

Letting me kiss you? Kissing me back? Kissing me back so passionately it ruined me—ruined me, damn you—for all other kisses?

"All of it," he murmured.

He leaned in a little closer and the heat of his body flowed over her skin, carrying with it his scent—laundry detergent, soap, and testosterone, she imagined. It was a scent that was all too familiar and entirely too pleasant for her peace of mind.

Danger, Will Robinson, her brain shouted. *Step back!*

Don't be stupid, her body argued. *Jump him!*

Oblivious to her inner turmoil, he raised his eyes to hers and asked, "Do you ever think about…how things might have been between us if I hadn't ruined everything?"

Violet blinked up at him. Well, that was a question she certainly hadn't been expecting. "Do you?"

His gaze dropped to her mouth before lifting to her eyes once more. There was only an inch or so separating their bodies, their mouths, and from the hot, dark look he was currently pinning her with, he realized it, too.

"I think about it all the time," he said, his voice even lower and raspier than usual. "It wasn't all a lie, you know. I often wonder if you'd ever let me make it right."

Sweet Christ, was he asking her to give him another chance? To…*date* him?

Her heart jumped up and down, squealing girlishly, while her brain reminded her what it felt like to be kidnapped and tied to a chair. And not even in the remotely fun and kinky way.

Stupid, *stupid* heart.

Violet cleared her throat again. "I don't believe in looking backward," she said in her best shrink voice. "There's nothing for you to make right. I accept your apology."

One corner of his mouth lifted and he reached for her, but she jerked back before he could make contact. There was no way she could keep her emotional shields up if he touched her. "We can go our separate ways now, and you have nothing left to feel guilty about," Violet added as sternly as she could muster.

In other words, we're done here.

Take that, Stockholm syndrome!

He stared at her a long moment, his eyes searching hers. His expression gave nothing away, but the ever-so-subtle slump of his shoulders let her know her message had been received loud and clear.

Finally, he nodded and said, "I understand. Whatever you need, I'll give you, *kotehok*. Even if it's my absence."

And as he turned away from her and started to leave, she couldn't be sure, but she thought he added, "I'd do anything for you."

Chapter Two

The cherry on top of the shit sundae of Violet's day came in the form of a printed death threat.

There were a few things that bugged her about this death threat. First of all, it was the third one she'd received in the past week. One was bad enough, but three? Her would-be assassin was most likely harboring some obsessive-compulsive tendencies. She could probably help him sort that out if he made an appointment with her instead of threatening to *murder* her.

Second of all, the messages were getting redundant. They never really varied enough to keep things interesting. If he was going to send three separate notes, the least he could've done was get a little creative with the whole thing. Maybe instead of saying, for example, "I'm going to kill you," he could've hinted at *how* he planned to kill her. Or more importantly, *why* he planned to kill her. *Where* he planned to kill her would also be good to know, she supposed.

And last but certainly not least, this particular death threat contained an egregious error a third grader should've been able to spot. Why send a death threat if you didn't care enough to proofread it before delivery?

"Your dead," Violet muttered, tossing the latest death threat into her top desk drawer. "He clearly meant 'you're dead.'"

Lexa flipped her smooth auburn hair over her shoulder and

placed a bulging bag of fragrant Chinese food on the desk between them. "Yes, Vi, because *that's* what's most troubling about the death threat: Poor grammar."

As usual, Violet didn't appreciate her assistant's sarcasm. But since Lexa made sure the office ran like a well-oiled machine and Violet's coffee cup was never empty, she kept her mouth shut. In the grand scheme of things, what was a little snark and lack of respect for authority when the alternative was caffeine withdrawal?

"Don't you think it's time you called the police about those notes?" Lexa asked.

"I did call them," Vi began as she pulled a carton—*oh, yummy. Pot stickers*—out of the bag, "but there wasn't much they could do. They didn't find any fingerprints on the other notes, and there's no return address on the envelopes, so unless the threat escalates into something physical, they're pretty much staying out of it."

Violet didn't add that the detective she'd spoken with also insinuated that maybe she wouldn't be in this predicament if her psychiatric practice focused on human patients as opposed to supernatural ones.

Lexa let out a disgusted snort as she broke apart a set of chopsticks and dug into her lo mein. "Our tax dollars at work. Whispering Hope PD is totally useless."

Violet couldn't really disagree. Their little town had a great many things to offer: fantastic restaurants, a wide range of talented local artisans, an adorable, bustling downtown business district full of historic brownstones and interesting architecture. But to get cops that gave a crap about the supernatural community? For that you'd have to leave town.

"Do you think it could be one of your patients? That guy who peed on his wife certainly wasn't happy when he left here the other day," Lexa said, then snickered.

Violet sighed. "Lex, first of all, you're not supposed to know anything about that. I need you to at least *pretend* you're not retaining any confidential information when you're transcribing my notes. And second of all, Mrs. Richards has a highly complex relationship with her husband. It's no laughing matter."

Lexa arched a single brow heavenward in that annoying way only supremely cool people could ever accomplish. "Vi, her werewolf husband peed on her to mark his territory when he thought her co-worker was hitting on her. If I can't laugh about *that*, what can I laugh about?"

Vi could admit on some level—a deep, deep, way, *way* down level—that she'd had to choke back a giggle or two when Mrs. Richards had explained what happened with her husband. But she wasn't about to admit it *aloud*. She was a professional, after all.

"Technically," Violet began as she set the pot stickers aside and dove into a container of garlic shrimp, "he didn't pee *on* her. He was only trying to mark the area *around* her cubicle." It was just Mrs. Richard's crap luck that she'd been hit with some…splatter.

Again with the raised brow. "Did she or did she not end up with her husband's urine on her leg?"

"She did," Violet grumbled.

Lexa sucked a noodle back with dramatic flourish, then shot Violet a self-satisfied, told-you-so smirk. "I rest my case."

Violet fought back an eye roll. She needed to introduce Lexa to her friends Mischa and Harper. The three of them loved to be right more than any people Vi had ever met in her life. They'd all get along famously.

"To answer your question," Violet said, "no, I don't think Mr. Richards wants to kill me for suggesting he come in for additional therapy sessions to help curb his urges. He wasn't happy with me, but he's a decent guy. Ultimately, he'll come back because he loves his wife and wants to make her happy. Therapy will help with that. Killing me? Not so much."

But sadly, while she was reasonably certain Mr. Richards didn't want her dead, it wasn't entirely outside the realm of possibility that *another* one of her clients—or former clients—might not exactly wish her all the best.

Her current and former patients' mental stability ranged from fairly solid to kind of, well, *murder-y*, to everything in between. If she was any other therapist, she most likely would've hired a full-time bodyguard after receiving the first threat. But knowing vampires and shapeshifters tended to be *super* dramatic when they were feeling vulnerable or emotional (as everyone tended to be in therapy), she wasn't terribly inclined to take her would-be assassin too seriously. She'd only gone to the police hoping that her stalker had made some kind of rookie mistake that would lead to an easy arrest.

"So you're just going to ignore the whole thing?" Lexa asked.

Violet shrugged. "Yes. What would you have me do?"

Lexa stared at her like she'd just suggested they go skinny-dipping in the Hudson. In January. "Um…I dunno…maybe call Lucas? Or Harper?"

Violet wasn't an idiot. She'd thought about calling Lucas when she received the first note. As a cop who'd once been on the Whispering Hope PD's vampire crimes unit (and as a dude who just happened to also be a werewolf), Lucas Cooper was uniquely qualified to provide guidance on her current predicament. But since he was also an ex-boyfriend and Seven's current husband, to say calling Lucas felt a little *awkward* was like saying the Pacific was a *tad* moist.

And Harper was an amazing woman—a psychic, in fact—who ran a successful paranormal PI firm, so Violet had considered calling her as well. But Harper Hall's services were in high demand these days, and Violet hated to waste her time on a threat that would most likely never amount to anything.

Besides, she hadn't spoken to Lucas or Harper since the kidnapping. Since she'd last been with…

Don't go there, dumbass.

"Lucas and Harper are busy. I didn't want to bother them." Violet held up a hand in supplication as Lexa shot her an exasperated glare. "*Fine*. If anything else happens, I'll give them a call. Okay, *mom*?"

Lexa looked less than appeased, but eventually grumbled, "Fine. I *feel* like your mom sometimes, you know. Getting you to do something for yourself is like trying to herd cats."

Time for a subject change, Violet thought. "I'm sure it's all just a stupid prank anyway, which means I have bigger concerns. Such as, what should I wear to the wedding next weekend? The red dress?"

Lexa's pert little nose wrinkled like she'd just sniffed a pile of fresh dog crap. "Ugh. I still don't understand why you're even going."

If she was being totally honest with herself, it was kind of a mystery to Violet, too. Maybe she was a closet masochist?

But at least her sister had let her out of maid of honor duties. That would've been *way* worse than simply attending as a guest. She shuddered at the thought of having to throw a bachelorette party for her incredibly nitpicky sister. "She's my sister, Lex. I can't just skip it."

"Yes, you can," Lexa immediately shot back. "That kid has always been jealous of everything you ever had. You're telling me she would've fallen for *Darren* if you hadn't been with him first?" She rolled her eyes. "Please. He's hell and gone from her type. That marriage won't last a year. Hardly worth your time at the wedding. *Definitely* not worth the vintage red Versace."

Violet had always done her level best not to psychoanalyze her family. But it was damn near impossible to ignore that her little sister, Rose, harbored some resentment toward her. It was hard to say why, really. Maybe because Violet was old enough to remember their father and Rose wasn't? Violet had plenty of happy memories of the man, but he'd passed away shortly before Rose had been born.

Whatever the reason, from the moment ten-month-old Rose snatched five-year-old Violet's beloved teddy bear from her arms and shouted "Mine" with far more fervor than any baby should possess, Rose seemed to make it her life's mission to covet—then take—anything Violet owned. Her latest acquisition? Darren Whitley, Violet's grad-school boyfriend.

Truth be told, if given the choice, Violet would rather have that ratty old teddy bear back than Darren. She probably would've broken up with him eventually even if he and Rose hadn't...

"He screwed her in your house while you were upstairs sleeping, Vi."

Well, she was *thinking* "fallen in love," but Violet supposed Lexa's assessment of the situation was fairly accurate, too.

"I don't see how you can forgive either of them for that shit," Lexa muttered.

Violet shrugged. "The truth is, I moved on. Yes, it hurt at the time,"—stung like a bitch and damn near crippled her self-esteem for a short time, more accurately—"but in the long run, I'm better off without Darren. And Rose is my sister. I *have* to forgive her."

Or at least that's what her mother told her. Over and over and over again.

Thank God the entire Marchand family only got together on special occasions. It also helped that the lot of them had no problem getting drunk off their asses to tolerate said special occasions. Yep. Her sister's wedding was sure to have a well-stocked, open bar, and Violet had every intention of making certain her glass never stayed empty for long.

Lexa made an undignified sound and leaned over to dump her empty lo mein carton in the trash can behind Violet's desk. "At least tell me you're not going to this dumpster fire of an event stag."

Violet shuddered. "Jesus, no. And sit at the singles table with the weird co-workers and backwards second cousins no one else wants to sit with? Miles agreed to be my plus one."

Lexa shot her a wide-eyed look of horror, the likes of which Violet hadn't seen directed her way since The Great Perm Debacle of '08. (It had seemed like a good idea at the time, OK? Violet had no idea her fine hair couldn't handle the stress of a perm and that she'd end up looking like an electrocuted alpaca.)

"You can't go to your sister's wedding—where she's marrying your *ex*, the ex who *cheated* on you with *your sister*—with Mr. Pathetic Rebound!"

Violet scowled at her. "I've asked you repeatedly to stop calling him that! There is nothing at all wrong with Miles. He's a great guy."

Great was maybe an overstatement. But he was exactly what Violet needed in her life at the moment. Miles was mellow, cerebral, gentle, and safe. But even more important than all of that, he was *human*. 100% normal, average, *human*. God knew her brief dips into the supernatural dating pool had been epic fails.

Lexa stared at her, obviously dumbfounded. "Vi, he's an actuary with a comb-over! He's a fucking walking cliché!"

"Oh, come on," Violet cajoled. "It's not like you to be so shallow. What do you *really* have against Miles?"

Lexa crossed her arms over her chest and leaned back in her seat. "How much time do you have?"

Violet kept an eye roll to herself. "Give me your top three."

Lex wasted no time digging into the topic. "Well, first of all, I've met him at least a dozen times and he still calls me Lisa."

So he wasn't good with names. So what?

"And," Lexa went on, "no matter what you say, he can spew 40 random statistics about it that no one gives a crap about."

Occupational hazard, Violet imagined. Work with numbers and statistics all day and it was bound to bleed over into your small talk. Was it sometimes annoying? Sure. But it wasn't a deal-breaker.

"And his whole demeanor with me shifted when he found out I didn't go to college. From that point on, he talked down to me like I was a three-year-old. Face it, Vi, he's a pompous ass."

Violet frowned, remembering the mini rant he'd recently gone on about the "uneducated troglodytes who didn't possess a tenth of his intellect" who'd been promoted ahead of him at work. And then there was his refusal to tip service workers because "if they wanted to make more money, they should've stayed in school."

Hmmm. Lexa might have a point with the whole *pompous ass* thing.

But Lexa didn't see the whole picture, Violet reminded herself. Miles made her feel calm. In control. He didn't make her feel the crazy rush of soul-searing emotion that got her in such trouble with…*him*.

With *him* she'd always felt like she was spinning, falling, flying, crashing, drowning…it was all too much. Too intense. He'd made her all but desperate to get closer to him. That kind of passion was not something she ever needed to repeat. That kind of passion left a trail of emotional debris in its wake—scars on your soul when you lost it (or when it was dragged out of your life, as the case may be).

That would never be a problem with Miles. And that's what made him so perfect for her at the moment. In the future? Who could say, really? Maybe he wasn't Mr. Right. But he made a damn fine Mr. Right Now.

Lexa cocked her head to one side and narrowed her eyes on Violet. "Why are you *really* with Miles? You have to know you can do better than a guy like that."

Violet attempted to lift a single brow the way Lexa did, failed miserably, and said, "Who says I *want* to do better?"

Lexa's expression shifted into something that looked dangerously close to pity. "You do. At least you always *used* to. You wanted something better when you were dating—"

Violet shot her a sharp choose-your-words-carefully-because-I'm-your-boss-and-can-fire-your-ass glare that stopped Lexa in her tracks mid-sentence.

Lexa swallowed hard and finished on a mumbled, "He Who Shall Not Be Named."

Silence stretched out for a few blissful moments, but Violet knew it wouldn't last long. Logically, Lexa knew Violet would never fire her. Violet could barely operate her iPhone, let alone the scheduling and bill payment systems Lexa navigated so easily. And then there was the coffee to consider…

"So," Lexa began, carefully avoiding eye contact, "Have you heard from He Who Shall Not Be Named lately?"

Sure I have. He showed up at my house this morning while I was in my Star Wars pajamas and asked me if I wanted to date him again.

But admitting to *that* would open up a whole can of emotional worms that Violet just wasn't in the mood to deal with at the moment, so instead, she said, "Have I heard from the man who stalked me, fake-dated me to get information on a patient of mine he planned to kill, drugged me, kidnapped me, and tied me to a chair?"

The man whose hands I can still feel on my body if I think about it hard enough? The man whose kiss ruined me—completely ruined me—for all other kisses?

Lexa offered a weak smile. "Yes?"

"No," she lied.

Lexa's shoulders slumped at that. The poor girl couldn't help herself. She was a hopeless romantic. But Violet was a realist. And as she'd come to learn over the years, a realist was just a romantic who'd had the shit kicked out of her heart enough times to realize love was just not in the cards for some folks. A happily-ever-after ending with Nikolai just wasn't going to happen.

When Violet didn't say anything else, Lexa decided to press her luck. "Oh, come on. All of…*that business* was essentially just a misunderstanding. The Vampire Council wouldn't have let him go if he was a danger to anyone, and he never hurt you, did he?"

"No. He didn't hurt me," she admitted.

Lexa's eyes softened. "He made a mistake, Vi. He was confused. You know better than anyone what he was going through. Half your patients are ex-Sentry employees, for God's sake."

And each one was more damaged than the last, she thought sadly.

"You could always reach out to him, you know," Lexa cajoled. "I'm sure Mischa has his contact information."

Call him and be his pathetic little Stockholm-syndrome-having groupie again? She snorted. "I think not."

Lexa opened her mouth—no doubt to argue—but snapped it shut when the office phone rang. She held up her index finger, silently asking Violet to continue their conversation in a moment, and picked up the call on her Bluetooth headset.

Violet marveled at Lexa's quick switch from nagging, mom-like pest to uber-professional office assistant, but then starting noticing additional changes in her body language as the caller continued speaking. Lexa's spine stiffened as she listened, her gaze lifted to Violet's and widened, and her jaw clenched ever so slightly. Violet's stomach sank in response. Those subtle reactions from the usually poised Lexa were the equivalent of screaming and flailing in anyone else.

Great. Now what?

After what felt like a damn eternity, Lexa thanked the caller and disconnected. Taking a deep breath, she said, "That was your neighbor."

Violet felt a frown line grooving its way across her brow. "Mrs. Copely?"

Lexa gave a quick, terse nod. "She came home from the grocery and found your door wide open. The alarm was disabled."

The frown line grooved deeper. Violet *always* locked her door when she left for work, and her security system was state of the art. The thought of someone getting into her apartment was bad enough, but someone being able to bypass her security? Well, that was downright terrifying.

"And," Lexa continued, "she didn't go in, but it looked to her like the place had been trashed."

"Well…shit," Violet muttered. "I guess it'd be overly optimistic of me to assume this break-in was unrelated to my recent death threats?"

Lexa's lips flat lined. "Probably," she said, sarcasm dripping from her tongue like venom.

"I suppose I should call Lucas and Harper, after all."

"This is what I'm saying."

"Any chance you'll keep the 'I told you so' to yourself on this one?"

"None."

Violet sighed. "Yeah, I didn't think so."

Chapter Three

Observing a staff meeting at Harper Hall Investigations was a little bit like watching someone juggle running chainsaws. It was loud, nerve-jangling, and under the right set of circumstances, extremely messy.

Violet sat at the head of the conference room table in the office suite of Harper's building in downtown Whispering Hope, pretending it wasn't at all odd to be the only human in the room with absolutely no paranormal abilities whatsoever. But she was willing to admit to *herself* it was weird.

Like, *really* weird. The kind of weird that almost made her want to recant her earlier call for help.

Harper sat at the opposite end of the battered oak table with a pile of papers scattered haphazardly in front of her. There was a stubby pencil that looked like a hungry wolverine had been gnawing on it tucked behind her ear and tangled in her gold-tipped brown curls.

In her faded jeans with giant holes in the knees and a T-shirt that read, "Strangers have the best candy," Harper looked less like a successful business owner and more like a college student heading into finals week. Or a frat party. Next to Harper, Violet felt like a grandma in her pencil skirt, cardigan sweater set, and tidy French twist.

Harper's husband, Noah Riddick, stood behind his wife protectively, arms crossed over his chest. And now that she thought about it, Violet wasn't sure she'd ever seen Riddick sit down. He was always wherever Harper was, on high alert, ready to tear apart anything that got too close to his wife. It'd be romantic if he wasn't such a terrifyingly imposing man.

If she had to guess by looks alone, Violet would say Riddick was an MMA fighter who posed for Calvin Klein ads in his spare time. But in actuality, he was, like Nikolai, a *dhampyre*, possessing strength, intelligence, and agility far superior to mere mortals like herself. His freakish good looks—the sexily disheveled black hair, the knife-edged cheekbones, the startling midnight-blue eyes, flawless olive skin—were just a happy genetic accident.

Lucas sat next to Vi with his wife, Seven, on his lap. And while Riddick never seemed to stop guarding his wife, Lucas, it would appear, was incapable of not touching his. It was sweet and kind of disgusting all at the same time.

Seven was Riddick's sister, and every bit as genetically blessed as her brother, both in supernatural talent and physical attributes. Her delicate, dark beauty was a perfect foil to Lucas's tousled blond, intense hotness. If she had to slap the title of supernatural Barbie and Ken on one couple, it would *for sure* be Lucas and Seven.

Across from Lucas and Seven, leaning negligently in his chair while drumming on the table with his thumbs to music only he could hear, sat Benny Scarpelli, one of Harper's investigators. Benny was a halfer, a somewhat unfortunate combination of vampire and wererat. He wasn't a bad guy, but his presence always made Violet check to make sure her blouse was fully buttoned, as she was pretty sure he was praying for a wardrobe malfunction.

Harper glanced up from the mess in front of her and said to Lucas, "Did the cops find anything useful?"

Lucas shoved a hand through his hair and sighed. "Do they ever? Once they heard it was Vi's house, they pretty much phoned it in from there. Cunningham—you remember him, right, Benny?—said she deserved whatever she got for working with the bloodsuckers."

At least Cunningham had the nerve to say it aloud, rather than hinting at it like the cop Violet had met with about the threats. She knew she should be angered by that kind of blind bigotry, but in all honesty, she was so used to it that it barely phased her anymore. Associates in the academic community, her parents, men she'd dated…they'd all made similar comments.

She hadn't really ever expected the police to find much, anyway. Their visit to her home had been less than comforting.

It had taken two police detectives and a small team of CSIs about two hours to collect a miniscule amount of evidence and coat every surface of her home in grimy black fingerprint dust. On their way out, they'd offered Violet a few platitudes about doing "everything in their power" to determine who'd broken into her home and destroyed many of her belongings. Their best advice? Try not to worry.

Riiiggghhhttt.

Benny let out a disgusted snort. "Cunningham. I hate that motherfucker. Dirty as shit. You can bet *nothing* will ever come of that investigation." He made air quotes around *investigation.*

Harper frowned. "What about you, Lucas? Did your wolfy senses pick up anything?"

Lucas frowned right back at her. "For future reference, werewolves don't like to be referred to as 'wolfy' anything. And all I can say for sure is that it was a vampire. I could smell it."

A chill skated down Violet's spine. She'd suspected as much, but *knowing* her death threats and trashed apartment were courtesy of one of nature's most perfectly designed predators was a whole other level of creep factor.

"Any visions, babe?" Riddick asked, laying his hands on his wife's shoulders.

Violet perked up. Harper had been one of Sentry's most gifted psychics. If anyone could find her supernatural stalker quickly and painlessly, it was Harper.

"Nope," Harper said. "Nada. I'm not surprised, though.

Anything the perp might've left behind for me to get a hit off of was ruined by the cops. The place looked like a herd of water buffalo had trampled through there by the time they were done with it."

And *splat* went her hope of the whole thing ending quickly and painlessly.

Fucking hope. You got me again, you miserable bitch.

Seven leaned forward and grabbed one of the photos Harper had taken of Violet's destroyed apartment. The photo was of the message that had been scrawled across her living room wall with blood-red spray paint. "I'm not a grammar expert," she began casually, "but I'm pretty sure that should say 'you're dead', not 'your'."

"I know, right?" Violet said, doing a palms-up what-the-fuck gesture. "It's troubling, isn't it?"

Seven nodded. "I hate stupid people."

"I hate death threats more," Lucas murmured. "Did you notice anything while we were there, beautiful?"

Seven glanced back at the photos dispassionately. "The amount of stuff destroyed suggests he was doing more than just trying to send a message. The person who did this was angry. Out of control. Emotional."

Violet swallowed hard, not liking the sound of *that* at all, but

Lucas grinned like a fool. "Very good observation," he said to Seven. "The PI exam isn't going to be a challenge for you at all."

Seven's blue eyes softened as she smiled at her husband, and suddenly, Violet felt like an intruder in what had just become their own little world. She turned away when Lucas cupped his wife's neck and planted what looked to be a knee-weakening kiss on her waiting lips.

Violet couldn't see it but she heard that the kiss went on for another moment or two. She shifted uncomfortably in her seat.

Call your ex-boyfriend and his new wife, who also happens to be an ex-patient, for help, she thought wryly. How awkward can it possibly be?

Pretty damn awkward as it turned out.

"Jesus," Riddick grumbled. "Why don't you just gouge my fucking eyes out, huh? It'd hurt less than watching this."

Graphic and overly dramatic, but also kind of true, Violet thought.

It wasn't that she begrudged Lucas and Seven their happiness. God knew they deserved it and had worked their asses off for it.

She supposed she was just jealous. Not of Lucas, of course. She wasn't fool enough to think a relationship between her and Lucas ever would've worked out; he was obviously made for Seven. But the partnership, friendship, trust, adoration, love (not to mention lots and lots of sex) Seven and Lucas had? Well, that was something rare that Violet had yet to ever experience, and she wanted it more than she was willing to admit aloud.

"You should've seen them at Vi's house," Harper said. "They're like a couple of teenagers. Can't you two keep your hands off each other for a freakin' minute?"

"Yes," Seven said at the same time Lucas said, "No."

Then Lucas added, "Don't shit on my joy because you guys have become an old, boring married couple with a dried-up sex life."

Harper looked him dead in the eye and brushed a curl off her forehead with her middle finger.

"Classy," Lucas said dryly. "And mature, as always."

Benny snorted. "Dried-up sex life? You obviously didn't hear them in the bathroom earlier. Swear to Jesus, after what I heard, I don't think I can ever go in there again without blushing."

Harper's head whipped around and she glared up at her husband. "You said no one was in the office to hear us!"

He grinned down at her, completely unrepentant. "No, I said no one *important* was in the office to hear us."

She narrowed her eyes on him. "You'll pay for that later, mister."

His grin grew and Violet fought back another jealous sigh. It'd been way too long since she'd gotten laid. She counted back. Shit…had it been a *year*?

That settled it. She was done with celibacy. No more coveting other peoples' sex lives, she thought. Maybe she'd even consider having sex with Miles.

She waited for excitement, happiness, anticipation, nervous butterflies…*something* to hit her at the thought of sex with Miles. It never did.

Great, Violet thought sourly. She'd probably waited so long to have sex that she was dying below the waist. Dried up like Sahara sand. If she didn't do something soon, she'd find herself wanting to adopt a bunch of cats and knit horrid little outfits for them.

Violet was jerked from her musings when Benny asked, "Hey, what about Hotness? Can she do anything to help figure out who might be after Vi?"

Harper shook her head. "Mischa and Hunter are busy jumping through hoops for the adoption agency. I didn't want to bother them, but we will if we have to."

Violet imagined adoption agencies didn't hand babies over to *regular* vampires without a litany of tests and obstacles, let alone to Mischa and Hunter, two of the most powerful vampires in the country. But since they could technically compel the officials to do whatever they wanted, Violet had to applaud their willingness to follow the process without cheating.

Lucas cleared his throat. "I'm going to go ahead and point out the elephant in the room. There's kind of an obvious suspect that no one seems to be mentioning."

Violet pulled in a sharp breath. Jesus. Her day sucked bad enough as it was. She *really* didn't want to talk about Nikolai again.

Harper cocked her head to one side. "You mean the hot Russian?"

"Whoa," Riddick said, holding up a hand. "You think *that* guy's hot?"

She blinked up at him. "Duh. I'm married, not dead."

He frowned down at her as Lucas snickered. Harper shot him a sharp look and said, "I wouldn't sound so smug over there, Wolfy. Seven agrees with me. Don't you, Seven?"

Seven nodded. "His features are definitely aesthetically pleasing. His body's very fit."

"Whoa," Lucas said, sounding aggrieved.

Benny shrugged. "If I was a chick, I'd do him."

"Not helping, man," Lucas said at the same time Riddick said, "Shut the fuck up."

Violet's mind drifted as the group continued to debate the level of Nikolai's hotness. She didn't add her opinion to the discussion, but Nikolai was *so* much more than *aesthetically pleasing* that she wondered if Seven needed to get her eyes checked.

The first time she saw him, she'd been stunned speechless, which, in her case, was kind of a blessing. She had a tendency to blurt out something embarrassing around really attractive men. (She had a vague memory of drunkenly telling Riddick he was so hot he made her ovaries hurt when she first met him. He was kind enough to pretend it'd never happened, though.)

Violet had met Nikolai outside the coffee shop around the corner from her Saturday morning yoga class. She'd just left the building and rounded the corner when she glanced down at her phone to read a text from Lexa. She looked back up just in time to run face-first into a brick wall.

"Son of a bitch!" she gasped as searing-hot coffee splashed down the front of her black tank top and yoga pants.

That's when the man in front of her cleared his throat and she realized she hadn't run into a brick wall at all. No, it was much more humiliating than that. She'd done a face-plant into a strange man's chest and managed to splash her coffee not only all over herself, but all over him, too.

"OhChristI'msosorryIdidn'tevenseeyouthere!" she blurted.

He peeled his coffee-soaked gray T-shirt away from his skin and smirked down at her. Way, way, down, because wow, he was so tall the top of her head only came up to his shoulder. And that's when whatever else she was going to blurt at him next escaped her.

Holy hell, he was perfect. Like Hollywood actor, Armani model *perfect*. And she'd just poured hot coffee all over him.

Awesome.

Those perfect pale green eyes of his moved over her face before sliding down her body, and damned if she couldn't actually *feel* the weight of his gaze on her. His brow furrowed in concern. "Are you alright?"

I've been rendered dumb and mute by a hot guy. Thanks for asking. How are you?

"Oh, I'm fine," she finally managed to spit out. "Are *you* okay?"

As if they weren't strangers, standing on Main Street in downtown Whispering Hope, he reached behind him, snagged the back of his wet T-shirt, and pulled it off over his head. He glanced down at his bare chest before looking back at her. "Barely left a mark. See?"

Violet about swallowed her tongue. So, so many muscles. How did a guy even get—two, four, six—*eight* visible abdominal muscles? Did he just live in the gym and lift weights all day?

He smiled. "Why? Do you want to work out with me?"

She blinked up at him. "Did I say that out loud?" she whispered.

He nodded, maintaining the smile.

Violet face-palmed. "Oh… *balls.*"

His answering chuckle was low and so sexy it made her forget she'd just humiliated herself—again. She cleared her throat.

"Again," she said, struggling to find her inner grown-up so she could stop acting like a hormonal pre-teen, "I'm really sorry. Is there anything I can do to make it up to you?"

And as soon as the words were out of her mouth, she wished she could snatch them back. She hadn't meant that to sound so suggestive. She'd only planned to pay for his cleaning bill or for a new shirt, not suck him off outside the coffee shop, for God's sake. But the look he pinned her with was hotter than the coffee she'd spilled all over him, and it let her know a replacement shirt wasn't first and foremost on his wish list.

His smile grew as he said, "Oh, I'm sure I can think of something."

Of course, she'd had no way of knowing at the time that the entire meeting had been carefully planned and plotted.

Harper pounded on the table with her fist, startling a gasp out of Violet. "Earth to Violet," she said, waving a hand in front of Violet's face. "Where the hell did you just go? You've got that dewy-eyed, dreamy look about you. You know, the one you get when we watch Captain Hook on *Once Upon a Time*."

Riddick crossed his arms over his chest. "Don't tell me. You find *him* hot, too."

"Yes," Violet, Harper, and Seven said in stereo.

"Oh, come on," Lucas whined. "That dude wears eyeliner."

Benny shrugged. "If I was a chick—"

"Do not finish that fucking sentence," Riddick growled.

Benny gave him a palms-up gesture. "Hey, I'm secure enough in my manhood to appreciate a good-looking dude. I mean, take you for instance, man. You're a *great*-looking dude. If I was a chick or gay or somethin'—"

Riddick took a menacing step toward him while Lucas let out a belly laugh that echoed through the room.

Benny swallowed hard and pulled his T-shirt away from his neck as if it were choking him. "I'll just be shutting the fuck up now," he muttered.

Harper banged on the table again. "Okay, enough already. Let's grow up, gentlemen. Shall we? Violet, have you heard anything from Nikolai lately?"

"He stopped by this morning to apologize for everything." She cleared her throat. "If he intended to hurt me, he could've done it then. I don't think this has anything to do with him."

"Mischa and Hunter were confident he wasn't a threat," Harper murmured. "Maybe they were wrong."

"He's not stalking Violet," Seven said confidently.

Lucas frowned. "He tried to kill you, Seven. Twice! He stalked and kidnapped Vi. It's not exactly a stretch to think he's targeted Vi again."

Violet often tried to forget that Seven had been Nikolai's target all those months ago. It made her friendship with Seven all the more awkward. Although, apparently *Seven* didn't find making friends with the man who tried to kill her awkward, so maybe Violet was just being a killjoy about the whole thing. Who knew?

"We should've killed that fucker when we had the chance," Riddick grumbled.

"Amen," Lucas said.

"He was confused," Seven argued. "Sentry essentially brainwashed him into thinking he had to kill all the other cleaners, but when push came to shove, he didn't kill me. He listened to what I had to say and turned himself over to the Council for their judgement."

"After he tried to *beat you to death*," Lucas said, enunciating each word clearly and slowly, annoyance clear in his tone.

Seven waved a hand dismissively. "It wasn't as dramatic as all that."

Violet blinked at her. Having had a front-row seat to the battle between Nikolai and Seven, she could say, without a doubt, that it most certainly *had* been as dramatic as all that. But, not seeing the point in rehashing that ancient history, she said, "He had plenty of opportunities to hurt me, and he never did. What motive would he possibly have for coming after me now?"

"Crazy people don't need no motive, doc," Benny said. "You should know that better than anyone."

"He's not crazy," Seven said, sounding frustrated. "Besides, he was with me when Violet's apartment was broken into today."

"Whoa," Lucas said at the same time Riddick said, "What the fuck?"

"He's my sparring partner," Seven said calmly, seemingly oblivious to why everyone was so surprised. She glanced back at Lucas. "I told you I was sparring every Tuesday."

Lucas shoved a hand through his hair again. "Yeah, but you didn't say you were sparring with *that* crazy motherfucker. I assumed you were sparring with Mischa or Riddick."

She shrugged. "Mischa's been busy, and Riddick pulls his punches with me. Nikolai is my best option."

Riddick scoffed. "Why, because he's not got a damn thing to do since there's no work in Whispering Hope for a trained killer, and because he's not afraid to throw a punch that'll actually *hurt* you?"

Seven looked relieved. "Yes, exactly. I'm glad you finally understand."

Riddick uttered a sound like maybe he was choking and opened his mouth to say something, but Lucas silenced him by raising a hand. He turned to his wife. "Baby," he began, taking her hand, "you remember how you wanted me to tell you when your communication skills needed some improvement?"

Seven's brow furrowed. "Yes."

"This is one of those times."

"Oh," she mumbled. "Sorry."

"No worries," he answered, giving her hand a squeeze. "Next time just tell me when you plan to spend time with the guy who kidnapped Vi and tried to kill you, okay?"

"Wow," Harper said as Seven nodded her agreement. "Sometimes I forget how weird we all are." Then she gave her head a hard shake and added, "Anyhoo, it sounds like Nikolai had an alibi for when Vi's place was trashed, so I'll question him just to be thorough, but I'm not liking him as a suspect at this point. So, let's all lay off the poor guy for now, okay?"

Everyone agreed. Some agreed more…grumbly than others (*cough*Riddick*cough*), but they all knew better than to argue with Harper.

Violet could've hugged Harper in that moment. She'd been nearly overwhelmed with the desire to take Seven's side and defend Nikolai, which was just beyond embarrassing, and kind of pathetic, really. Maybe she hadn't totally beaten her Stockholm syndrome into submission after all.

"That means that until we figure this thing out," Harper said, "Vi, you're going to need a bodyguard."

Violet cringed, visions of a dour-faced Kevin Costner in that awful '90s movie running through her mind. "Do you really think that's necessary?"

"I don't believe in taking chances. And besides, if this person is stalking you, stalkers almost always escalate at some point. I'd rather you not be alone if that happens."

Violet felt a little sick to her stomach at the thought of what kind of *escalation* her stalker might hit her with next. What was a step up from trashing her apartment? Not liking any of the possibilities that popped into her head, she agreed to allow Harper to assign her a bodyguard for the foreseeable future.

"Just so you know," Violet said, "I'm going out of town for a wedding this weekend. What if I can't get an additional plus one?"

"Dump your date," Harper fired back immediately. "Take your bodyguard as your plus one. We'll need to clear your date of suspicion before you spend any time alone with him, anyway."

Violet laughed out loud at the thought of *Miles* being dangerous in any way, but Harper merely shrugged and said, "Like I said, I don't like to take any chances."

Riddick glanced down at his wife. "You want me to go with her?"

Violet perked up. Showing up with someone who looked like Riddick on her arm would probably offer her immunity from having to sit at the singles table *ever again.*

Harper sighed. "Maybe? I'm not sure. I need to check everyone's schedules. In the meantime, Benny, can you take Violet home and stay with her until I know who I can post with her full time?"

Benny jumped up, looking way happier than Violet was strictly comfortable with. "Hell, yeah!" he said. "I'm on her."

Violet did her best to avoid a sour expression as she hoped he meant he was on *it*, not *her*.

"Great," Harper said, smiling sweetly. "Now that *that's*

settled, Riddick, can I get you to run out and pick up something for me?"

Was it just Violet's imagination, or was there something decidedly *sinister* about Harper's sweet smile?

Chapter Four

It wasn't Nikolai Aleyev's first kidnapping.

His years as a cleaner with Sentry were spent doing the jobs no one else wanted or was willing to do, and that training had made him a rather adept kidnapper.

He knew that zip ties were a hell of a lot more practical and effective than metal cuffs. He knew several combinations of household products that could easily be made into do-it-yourself chloroform. He understood that while efficient, panel vans drew too much attention from the authorities to be used as a getaway vehicle. Nondescript sedans with large trunks worked best. (Nikolai was partial to the newer model Ford Taurus, which had a trunk large enough to transport two average-sized human bodies.)

But what he'd never known, and something his training couldn't have prepared him for, was how it felt to be the *victim* of a kidnapping.

That was something he hadn't experienced until today.

After his complete and utter disaster of a conversation with Violet, the day had moved along ordinarily enough. He'd gone to work at the construction site in the morning. He finished the new roof on the Johnsons' summer rental in under two hours, so his boss was particularly pleased with him and even let him go home early.

After work, he stopped by the gym to spar with Seven for a

couple of hours. It had been a good workout. They hadn't even broken any of each other's bones this time, which meant their control was improving.

Not that it really mattered. As *dhampyres*, their wounds always healed quickly and never amounted to anything more than a minor annoyance. But still, control was something Sentry hadn't really been known for teaching. Being able to master a task Sentry hadn't encouraged made Nikolai feel good. Almost like he was telling them to fuck off.

And Seven being able to control her right hook was a blessing for his profile. He wasn't sure how many more times his nose could be broken without the cartilage turning to mush.

After the gym, he'd done his usual check-in with his Vampire Council-appointed parole officer, or, as Seven liked to say, his babysitter. His PO's sole purpose was to ensure Nikolai's moods and behaviors were stable, and that he didn't feel like murdering anyone. Today, Nikolai had received a near-glowing report on his mental health and emotional stability.

He hadn't mentioned his conversation with Violet to his PO. The guy probably would've offered an *entirely* different report on his emotional stability if he knew just how thoroughly Nikolai's hopes for reconciliation with Violet had been crushed.

But after that, he'd showered, eaten dinner, and gone to bed. Nothing out of the ordinary at all.

Until someone with a left hook like a freight train broke into his house, threw a bag over his head, and tossed him into the trunk of a '69 Mustang.

Sadly, the trunk of a classic Mustang was nowhere *near* as roomy as that of a Taurus.

Nikolai had fought back against his attacker for a while. Until he realized who it was, of course. After that, he assumed the whole thing was some kind of trial his PO and the Council had devised to test his resolve to live like a normal person.

Like someone who hadn't once been a serial killer for hire.

So, Nikolai went against every instinct he had and stayed compliant as he was pulled from the trunk, dragged into a building, and forced down onto a metal folding chair.

When the bag was ripped off his head, he found himself blinking up at Harper Hall.

"You know," Riddick began casually as he moved from behind the chair toward his wife, "I'm not an expert on relationships and shit, but I think most wives ask their husbands to pick up stuff like milk and eggs on their way home."

Harper crinkled up her nose. "Sounds boring as hell. Aren't you glad you're with me instead of one of those other wives?"

"Abso-fuckin'-lutely," he answered, turning to drop a quick

kiss on her mouth.

"Thanks for picking…*this* up for us, babe," she said. "We have plenty of milk and eggs, by the way."

He grinned at her. "Good to know. Your mom has the munchkin until tomorrow?"

"Yep. Like usual, she ripped her from my arms and told me not to show my face in her house until then," Harper said with a scowl.

His grin turned predatory. "Hmmm. Whatever will we do with the house all to ourselves?"

Obviously the thought of what they could do to each other during the hours that Harper's mother was caring for their daughter hadn't occurred to her, because her mouth dropped open and she let out a breathy, "Oh, wow."

Seven stepped into Nikolai's line of vision and frowned down at him. "He has a split lip! Was that really necessary, Riddick?"

"Yes," Riddick said without hesitation.

Seven shot Riddick a dirty look that had him shrugging in confusion at his wife as if to innocently ask, "What? What did I do?"

Harper just rolled her eyes while Seven said, "I'm so sorry, Nikolai. Are you OK?"

Nikolai felt an odd tightening in his chest as she continued to stare down at him, concern etched all over her pretty face. When was the last time anyone had fretted over his safety and well-being? Before his parents died and he was sold to Sentry? Probably. He couldn't even remember.

"I'm fine, *Семь*," Nikolai told her. "No one will hurt me."

Riddick made a rude noise in the back of his throat. "First of all, you tried to kill my sister. Twice. So, you don't get to have a cutesy nickname for her. Second of all, you're awfully calm and confident for someone I just pulled out of the trunk of Harper's car."

Seven crossed her arms over her chest and glared up at her brother. "*Семь* is just Russian for Seven. It's not a cutesy nickname. And if I can forgive him for trying to kill me, why can't you?"

Riddick set his jaw mulishly. "You wouldn't let me kill him when I wanted to. Fine. I can deal with that. But I don't have to *like* him, and I don't have to be nice to him."

Harper waved a hand dismissively and shoved Seven and Riddick out of her way. "Just ignore them, Nikolai. I didn't have Riddick bring you here to talk about your friendship—or whatever you guys call getting together every so often to beat the crap out of each other—with Seven."

Riddick dragged a chair over in front of Nikolai's. Harper smiled her thanks up at him as she straddled the chair backwards.

When she turned her smile on Nikolai, it sharpened, and he had to fight the urge to recoil.

Harper had been a seer with Sentry. Seers always made him a little nervous. Nikolai could lie like a fucking champ, and could even control his heartrate and blood pressure, which was the best way to sell a lie to a *dhampyre* or vampire. But there was nothing anyone could do to block a seer. With one touch, they could see through any lie, any cover, any variation of the truth.

His whole life was a lie. He could hide who he really was from his employer, his PO, and even from Seven. But he couldn't hide it from someone like Harper.

The truth that everyone failed to accept was that he was exactly who Sentry trained him to be: a killer. Irredeemable. Total unworthy of concern from someone as good and kind as Seven.

Or Violet.

Not that it mattered. Violet had made her feelings—or complete lack thereof—for him abundantly clear that morning. The ache in his chest, the constant feeling that he'd lost something vital to his survival—something he'd never really had, as it turned out—had plagued him ever since.

Just another side effect of his time with Sentry he'd have to learn to live with, he supposed.

"So," Harper began, dragging the word out for several extra

syllables, "we have a bit of a situation, Nicky. Can I call you Nicky?"

He offered her his sternest glare—a glare that had made grown men damn near piss their pants. "Not if you expect me to answer."

Harper shrugged, seemingly impervious to his glare. "Someone is stalking one of my friends," she said. "Trashed her house. Left her a few death threats."

Nikolai felt his brow furrow. "I'm not stalking anyone."

He didn't add that he'd never be stupid enough to leave anyone death threats, either. Why the hell would you ever want to *warn* the person you intended to kill that you intended to kill them? That'd just make it easier for them to evade you and make your job harder.

But somehow he figured that additional information wasn't something Harper needed—or wanted—to hear, so he kept it to himself.

Harper nodded. "Seven believes you."

But you don't, Nikolai thought. Not that he blamed her. If the situation was reversed, he wouldn't believe her, either.

Riddick cracked his knuckles. "This is taking forever. Why don't I just beat it out of him?"

Seven hauled off and punched her brother in the arm. Nikolai almost winced in sympathy. Like her brother, Seven hit like a freight train. Riddick would be feeling that punch all night.

"She hasn't even asked him anything yet," Seven hissed as Riddick scowled and rubbed the spot where she'd punched him. "That's not how interrogation works and you know it!"

"Don't make me send you kids out of the room so that the grown-ups can talk," Harper said, not even a hint of irritation in her voice. Obviously this kind of familial bickering wasn't foreign to her.

Seven and Riddick mumbled half-hearted apologies, and Harper shook her head fondly, then refocused her attention on Nikolai. "This friend of mine that's being stalked? It's someone you've stalked before, Comrade. Why should I believe you're innocent this time?"

Violet. She was talking about Violet.

The thought of someone threatening Violet, of her being in danger, made every dark, violent urge he'd ever had rise up from deep within him. "Is she safe?" Nikolai asked through gritted teeth, completely unable—despite his best efforts to control himself—to keep the anger and heat from his tone.

Harper tipped her head to the side and studied him through slightly narrowed eyes for a moment. "Hmm. It's really *not* you, is it?"

"God damn it," he gritted out. "Just fucking tell me. Is she safe or not?"

"Hey," Riddick growled, turning his barely pent-up rage back on Nikolai. "Use that tone with her again and I'll rip your spleen out through your nose, asshole."

Nikolai ignored him, keeping his attention on Harper, who merely offered him a benign smile and said, "She's fine. For now. But she needs a bodyguard until we figure out who's after her."

She's fine. Nikolai let those words sink in, and when they did, he let out a relieved breath. Thank God. "Who's with her now?"

"Benny," Seven answered.

And just like that, his relief was smashed into a million fucking pieces. He spit out every Russian curse he knew in one long, irritated breath. "Jesus Christ, you left her safety to the *halfer*? What the hell were you thinking? He can't look after *himself*, let alone Violet."

Harper shrugged, completely unfazed by the violence in his tone. "I was *thinking* I didn't have anyone else who could do the job. But now, I might have an idea."

"Tell me," he growled.

She leaned forward and her grin—which was starting to *really* piss Nikolai off—grew even wider, almost predatorial in a way that made him decidedly…edgy. "I will. But first I have one question for you."

Chapter Five

"Good news, babe. I found you a bodyguard."

Violet sighed with relief as she watched Benny toss peanuts up into the air, then try to catch them with his gaping mouth. He missed more than he succeeded. "That's great," she said into the phone. "Thank you so much for doing this."

Harper chuckled. "Don't thank me just yet. You might not be entirely happy with my choice."

Violet glanced over at Benny. Could her new bodyguard really be any worse than the guy who'd just spent the last hour letting greasy peanuts hit her white sofa while trying to explain to her which Kardashian was "the smart one?" All while she cleaned up her apartment and he *not once* offered even the slightest bit of help? The mind boggled at such a notion. "I'm sure it'll be fine. Who is it?"

"Let's just say it was a…nontraditional choice."

Violet frowned. "Oh. Is it a woman? Seven maybe? Because I'm totally OK with taking Seven to the wedding as my date. I'm pretty sure half my family suspects I'm a lesbian anyway, and she's probably hot enough to get me out of the singles table for life."

"No, it's not Seven, but it *is* someone she recommended," Harper evaded.

"Harper, you're starting to make me nervous."

Another laugh. "Yeah, I get that a lot. He should be there any minute. Just keep an open mind, OK?"

She was about to remind Harper that she was a psychiatrist who specialized in treating paranormal patients, and that minds didn't really *get* more open than Violet's. But the doorbell rang, so Violet decided to hold her tongue for the moment.

"Hang on a second, Harper," she said.

"Sure thing, babe. Remember, open mind. Really, really open, OK? Like, *wide*-open, free-range, huge-Montana-cattle- country open, you know?"

"All right, all right," Violet muttered, swinging the door open.

Violet took one look at the man who was standing in her doorway, holding a duffel bag, looking like he intended to stay a while, and slammed the door shut in his face. To Harper she said, "No way in hell."

Harper sighed. "I told you to keep an open mind."

"There's open and then there's…*gaping* like a giant *wound*, Harper," Violet hissed. "I can't have him here!" She started pacing the length of her living room. "Oh my God, I can't take him with me to my sister's wedding!"

Jesus, just the thought of him—all big and tall and disturbingly good-looking and smelling so delicious—in her space, her domain…no. It couldn't happen. She'd just kicked her Stockholm syndrome, for God's sake! She couldn't invite him back into her life now!

Crap, she was starting to hyperventilate just thinking about it.

"Whoa, doc, you gotta calm down," Benny said, then pressed something into her hand. "Here, take a few deep breaths into this bag."

Violet shot him a grateful look and shoved her mouth and nose into the bag, inhaling deeply. Everything would've been fine at that point if the bag Benny handed her hadn't been full of mini powdered doughnuts.

Slowly pulling the bag away from her face, she fixed Benny with what she could only hope was a death glare. He merely chuckled and swiped a bit of powdered sugar off her nose with his pinky.

"Well, doc," he said, "you look like you've been snorting coke, but at least you're not hyperventilating anymore. You're welcome."

And with that, he swaggered back over to her couch, flopped onto his back, and reached for her remote, presumably to pick up where he left off in his reality TV marathon.

"Look, Vi," Harper began, "I know that working with him isn't going to be super comfortable for you."

Violet snorted. Comfortable? All bow down to Harper Hall, Queen of Understatement.

"And if after you hear me out, you still want to send him away, I can send Riddick over to take Benny's place. Hell, I'm sure I can even convince him to fawn all over you at the wedding and pretend to be the best date ever."

Violet let out a deep, relieved breath. Well, thank God. She had an out. All she had to do was hear Harper out, then politely decline and have her send Riddick over. Done and done.

"This isn't the first time I've assigned bodyguards to a client," Harper said. "And every time, I have one question I ask the potential guard. All I want to know from them is this: Would you take a bullet for the person I'm asking you to guard?"

Wow, that question certainly put the whole bodyguard thing into perspective. She'd never really considered the possibility of someone getting hurt while trying to protect her. More honestly, she hadn't *let* herself consider that possibility. It was just too horrible to fathom.

"So," Harper went on, "you had no shortage of people who would protect you, which is nice. But when I asked Riddick the question, he shrugged and said, 'I guess so.'" She chuckled. "Not really the level of commitment I was looking for, you know? Seven, on the other hand, immediately said she'd take a bullet for you, and I believed her 100%. But trust me when I tell you that you *would not* want to deal with Lucas and Riddick if something were to happen to Seven while she was trying to protect you. The ensuing alpha male drama and angst would be absolutely *exhausting*."

Violet had to agree with Harper on that one. Between Seven's husband and her big brother, Violet couldn't really say who was more protective, mostly because they were both *scarily* protective of their girl.

And while she totally appreciated Seven's willingness to take a bullet for her, Violet wouldn't ever put her former patient in the line of fire. Seven had worked too hard for her happily-ever-after to have anything ruin it now.

"Mischa and Hunter would do it in a heartbeat," Harper said, "but I didn't want to ask them. With everything they're going through to adopt, I didn't want to put anything else on their plate. And I assume Lucas would also take a bullet for you, but I had to ask him the question three times because he was too busy staring at his wife's legs to comprehend. So, that automatically ruled him out. ADD and bodyguards *do not* mix."

Violet closed her eyes and pinched the bridge of her nose. She had a sinking suspicion where Harper was going with this train of thought and she didn't like it. Not. One. Bit. But still, she couldn't stop herself from asking, "And what did Nikolai say when you asked him?"

"He didn't even hesitate. He said, 'I would die for her.'"

I'd do anything for you.

How was it possible that those words filled her with unfathomable joy and unmitigated dread all at the same time? She was in trouble, and he was willing to do anything to protect her. It was humbling. And exciting. But given their history together, could she really believe he wasn't just as big a threat to her well-being as her stalker was?

Violet let out a frustrated growl. "And I suppose you believe him?"

"I do. He was all clenched jaw and flashing eyes when he said it. I'm convinced he meant every word. It was actually kind of hot."

Of *that* Violet had no doubt.

"But, like I said, it's up to you, doc. I can send him away and put Riddick on the job in his place. I have every confidence that Riddick would keep you safe while I figure out who's after you. But honestly? If I was in your Prada pumps? I'd choose Nikolai."

Oh, God. This whole crazy-pants nightmare of a plan was actually starting to make *sense*. What the hell was the matter with her? "Harper, why would he want this job? You talked to him. Did he give you any clue as to why he'd be willing to"—gulp—"take a bullet for me?"

"I have my theory," she hedged. "But I don't think it really matters. I believe he wants to protect you. Whether that's because he feels guilty about how he treated you in the past, or because he has some kind of other feelings for you…what difference does it make? Whatever his feelings and reasons are, I think you should use them to stay safe."

Use *his* feelings for a change. That was an interesting concept. Considering all he'd put her through, maybe protecting her now was kind of the least he could do.

"And there's something else I think you need to take into consideration," Harper said.

"What's that?"

"Well, I can't be certain," Harper added, her voice taking on a teasing note, "but I'm betting he looks *fuck hot* in a suit, and since he'd be your date at the wedding, I'm thinking that'd be an added bonus."

Now, that just wasn't playing fair at *all*.

Violet groaned. "Harper, if I agree to this, do you promise to make my case a priority and find this guy as quickly as possible?"

"Pinky swear, sister," she shot back.

And after another minute, the call was done and the deal was brokered, leaving Violet vaguely feeling like she'd just sold her soul to the devil.

When she opened her door, she found that Nikolai hadn't

budged. There he stood, duffel at his feet, arms above his head, crossed wrists braced on the top of her doorframe. She refused—*refused*, damn it—to notice the lovely things the position did for his triceps.

She had a million things she wanted to say to him. Conditions of this *arrangement* she wanted to lay out. Thoughts and feelings she wanted to make perfectly clear. But every word she could've uttered dried up under the intensity of those green eyes as he stared down at her.

So, in the interest of not blurting out anything embarrassing, she crossed her arms over her chest and stepped aside so he could come into her apartment.

He took his time picking up his bag and stepping inside, almost like he was giving her a chance to change her mind. But while he was polite enough to give her a little time to think, he went the complete opposite route with her personal space.

He walked into the foyer and stopped close enough to her that she had to crane her neck back to meet his gaze. The heat she felt rolling off him in waves and the clean, masculine scent of his skin made her stomach clench with the desire to wrap her arms around his waist and press her nose into the space where his neck and shoulder met.

It'd be his own stupid fault if she did, she thought. How *dare* he stand there looking so smug and strong and willing to take a bullet for her?

And still he stood there, staring down at her, waiting for…something.

"What is it?" she finally asked when she couldn't stand another second of tense silence.

Her mouth dried up and her tongue stuck to the roof of her mouth when he slid his fingertips under her hair and let them rest lightly on the back of her neck. With his thumb, he gently brushed something off her cheek.

Powdered sugar, she realized.

His eyes held hers as he slowly—so, *so* slowly—lifted his thumb to his mouth and licked off the powdered sugar. Her entire body clenched at the sight of his tongue swiping over his own skin.

Holy. Fuck.

"Delicious. You taste even better than I remember," he murmured before releasing her and walking away as if he hadn't just reduced her to a puddle of lust right there in her own damn foyer.

Well, the good news, she supposed, was that her lady bits hadn't dried up after all, as she had suspected earlier that day. The bad news? The man capable of awakening them was the last man in the world she should trust with her body—or her heart—ever again.

Yep. Seemed about right, given the day she'd had.

Chapter Six

She slammed the door in his face.

Violet would rather risk death than have him in her home. Not exactly a shot in the arm for his ego.

He didn't blame her, though. It wasn't like he'd done anything to ingratiate himself with her up until this point.

Maybe that was why he'd jumped at Harper's offer as quickly as he had. There'd been no hesitation on his part. And he wasn't even going to *try* kidding himself about it. The idea of possibly earning redemption for what he'd done to Violet? It was wildly enticing.

Almost as enticing as the woman herself.

Nikolai tossed his duffel bag on the couch next to the halfer, who appeared to be engrossed in some television program. Nikolai barely repressed a snort of disgust. *This* was the man responsible for Violet's safety until he'd arrived.

"Leave," Nikolai told him.

The halfer didn't take his eyes off the television as he answered, "I go when Harper tells me to go. Not a minute before."

Nikolai felt a tiny hint of grudging respect for the guy. Not too many men ever refused his direct orders.

Not ones who lived to talk about it, at least.

Violet cleared her throat and stepped in front of him. Her breathing and color were heightened, and she was glaring up at him with an intensity that suggested she wanted to tear him apart.

His little *kotehok* planned to sharpen her claws on his hide. The idea was *way* more enticing than it should have been, given their current circumstances.

"We need to talk," she said through gritted teeth.

He shrugged. "So talk."

Her eyes narrowed slightly. "Did Harper explain the situation to you?"

He shifted his eyes to the spray-painted death threat on her wall before meeting hers once again. "I'd say it's pretty clear."

He could've sworn she growled at that point. He couldn't say if it was his casual tone or his words that vexed her so. All he knew for sure was that a happy Violet was stunningly beautiful. But an angry Violet?

Hot. As. Hell.

"I *meant* that you're here to guard me until she can figure out who is threatening me," she hissed. "That doesn't give you the right to march in here and start issuing orders to my guests and…and touching me."

Ah. There it was. She was upset about the powdered sugar.

He couldn't really blame her for that. Honestly, he had no idea what had made him do it. Maybe he wanted to see if he still had the power to fluster her. He used to, before he fucked everything up.

And, if her dazed expression and heightened breathing in the doorway had been any indication, she wasn't as calm and cool around him as she'd like him to think she was.

Interesting.

"So…no touching?" he asked as innocently as he could manage.

She straightened to her full height, which still only put the top of her head at his shoulder. "No touching."

His fingers itched with the need to touch her again at the mere suggestion. "You didn't used to mind me touching you."

Her icy blue eyes darkened, making him regret the words immediately. He wasn't here to antagonize her. But the hostility radiating from this straight-backed, tense woman, who wasn't anything like the Violet he'd known, was seriously mucking up his best intentions.

He held up his hands in surrender as she opened her mouth, no doubt to deliver the verbal blast he so richly deserved. "Forget I said that. You win. No touching. If I can help it."

Her eyes narrowed and he hastened to add, "*Kotehok*, I'm to be your guard. I'll need to be close to you." God help us both. "I might touch you by accident." Or on purpose. His self-control was clearly shit where she was concerned.

She took a deep breath and he cursed himself for letting his gaze fall to her chest. The rise and fall of her breasts under the sweater she wore was damn near mesmerizing.

He was never going to survive being close to her and not touching her. He'd been a damn fool to volunteer for this job.

Time for full disclosure, he supposed. "Look, Violet, I am truly sorry this is happening to you. The last thing in the world I want to do is make you uncomfortable or make your life harder. I just really want to keep you safe. It's the least I can do." He bent at the knees so that they were at eye level. "Will you let me? Please?"

And just like that, her anger deflated. He saw it in those expressive eyes of hers, and in the way her shoulders dropped, no longer looking like they were attached to her ears. It was as if the truth and sincerity of his words melted all the starch out of her spine. Or, maybe the stress of the day was finally beginning to wear down her resistance.

Whatever it was, it was a victory and he'd take it.

She released a long, hard breath and rubbed her temple with one hand. "I don't know what's wrong with me today," she murmured. "I should be thanking you for volunteering to keep me safe and instead I'm arguing with you about stupid stuff."

Immediately forgetting the "no touching" rule, he grabbed her hand and squeezed her icy fingers with his own. "You've had a terrible, long day. Your behavior is completely normal. And you don't have to thank me for anything. I *want* to be here."

He *needed* to be here, if he was being honest with himself. He was fine with staying away from her when he thought it was what she needed, what was *better* for her. But now? She needed *him*, and he'd be damned if he'd ever let her down again.

Her eyes moved from her hand in his, up to his face. She looked apprehensive and maybe a little nervous, but he noticed she didn't try to pull her hand away. Not a huge victory, but a victory nonetheless.

Again, he'd take it.

"What about your new job?" she asked.

"You're my job right now."

Which was true. The Council had spoken to his PO and employer on his behalf and they'd granted him permission to stick with Violet as long as necessary.

Not that he wouldn't have done exactly what he was doing now *without* their permission. Breaking the rules seemed to be in his DNA. Anyone at Sentry who'd worked to reprogram him could most likely attest to that.

She swallowed hard and nodded. "Harper told me what you said about…dying for me," she said quietly. "Did you mean it?"

He'd said a lot of things to Harper, but Nikolai knew by her shy tone what she was getting at. She sounded so lost that he wanted to kill someone. Preferably whoever was threatening her, but at the moment, he wasn't feeling too picky. He'd gladly kill anyone who'd ever wronged her in her life.

And he wouldn't allow himself to think too hard about how *he* was, in fact, a person who'd wronged her.

Nikolai cleared his throat. "I did. I already told you, Violet. I'd do anything for you."

Her eyes flew to his, searching. Gauging his truthfulness, he knew. He let her look her fill. He had nothing left to hide from her. Everything he had—his body, his heart, his life—was hers if she wanted it.

It always had been. Since the moment they first met and she smiled at him, he was lost. She was sunshine and sweet dreams and hope. Everything he wasn't. Everything he'd ever wanted, but assumed he'd never have.

He wondered what the hell she saw when she looked at him. Killer? Kidnapper? Liar? A man she'd wanted at one point? Someone she could see any kind of future with?

She let out a little gasp and that's when he realized he was still holding her hand, absently running his thumb over her knuckles. At some point, he'd also tugged her closer. The scent of her shampoo—limes and coconuts—drifted up to him and his mouth started watering like Pavlov's fucking dog.

Violet's eyes dropped to his mouth. Her tongue snaked out, dragging along her bottom lip and Nikolai barely bit back a groan. She was killing him and she had no idea.

"Hey, Harper's getting impatient over here! You two gonna kiss, or what?"

Violet flinched at Benny's voice, which rang out like a gunshot in the otherwise quiet room. She jerked her hand out of his grasp and averted her eyes, looking guilty as hell.

Nikolai's hands went to his hips and he turned a glare on Benny, who was holding up his phone.

"You have Harper on speaker, don't you?" Violet asked, her voice breaking on the last word.

Benny nodded, his eyes bouncing between Nikolai and Violet like he was watching a ping pong match, not a trace of remorse in his expression. "Oh, yeah. You guys were way more interesting than my show. And when I told Harper what was going on, there was no way she was lettin' me hang up, you know?"

Nikolai turned back to Violet. "Can I throw him out now?"

"Yes, please," Violet said primly.

Benny's last words as Nikolai grabbed him by the collar and tossed him out the door were, "Aw, man, come on. That shit was just gettin' good."

Yes, Nikolai thought, *it sure was. And that's why I'm throwing your ass out.*

Chapter Seven

It took Violet nearly an hour of standing in front of her mirror doing deep breathing exercises and offering herself positive affirmations before she was able to calm down and accept her new reality.

She had a stalker who'd left her a few death threats and broken into her home. So what? Harper Hall was on the case, and Violet had yet to see a case that Harper and her team couldn't resolve quickly.

Until Harper solved the case, she had a live-in bodyguard. So what? She'd grown up with three sisters in a 700-square-foot apartment. Privacy wasn't essential to her survival.

She'd almost kissed her live-in bodyguard, who just happened to be the guy who'd kidnapped her and tried to kill one of her patients that one time. So...

Well, *that* one was a little harder to "so what."

Kissing Nikolai would be a bad idea. No, *bad idea* was an understatement. Kissing Nikolai was the *high priestess* of bad ideas. The bad idea to which all other bad ideas aspired to be when they grew up.

The bad idea that *couldn't happen*, under any circumstances.

Not ever again, anyway.

She needed to focus on keeping her Stockholm syndrome at bay, and her bodyguard had to focus on, well, guarding her body. It was just as simple as that.

I'd do anything for you.

"Gah," she muttered, taking a moment to splash some cold water on her face.

How the hell was she supposed to *not* kiss him when he was so close all the time, saying such perfect, heart-wrenching things, smelling like heaven, invading her personal space with all those taut, tan muscles that she just wanted to trace with the tip of her tongue …

Violet splashed more cold water on her face and didn't bother to stop it from dripping down into her shirt. At this point, she could use all the help she could get when it came to cooling off.

"It's just attraction. Chemistry," she told her reflection as she dabbed a few water droplets off her face with a hand towel. "Chemistry isn't everything. You can beat this…thing."

"What thing?"

Violet shrieked at the unexpected voice and whirled around, tossing her damp hand towel at the intruder like it was a grenade she'd just pulled the pin out of.

Nikolai stood in the doorway of her bathroom, stone-faced, hands on his hips. His gaze followed the hand towel as it smacked him in the center of his chest, then plopped to the floor at his feet. When his eyes lifted to hers once again, one of his dark brows lifted in confusion.

Violet closed her eyes and put a hand over her pounding heart, which seemed to be keeping time to a death metal song only it could hear. "Jesus Christ, you startled me!"

"And you didn't have anything better to throw at me than a towel?" He glanced behind her. "Next time someone sneaks up on you in the bathroom, go for the hair spray. Aim for the eyes. It's almost as effective as Mace."

She scowled at him. "Well, lucky for you, I didn't. I could've really hurt you."

And then he did something she'd never seen him do before. He laughed.

Flustered by that deep, rich, sex-soaked laugh and those damned dimples of his, Violet shifted her focus to brush a few invisible wrinkles off her blouse. She sniffed. "I fail to see why that's funny."

"You couldn't hurt me, *kotehok*," he said when his laugh had died down to a chuckle. But just when she was going to slam him with a retort about how women could be every bit as effective at self-defense maneuvers as men, he quietly added, "Not physically, anyway."

Her heart squeezed hard. To think maybe she had the same kind of power over *him* that he had over *her*? It was…well, it was terrifying, frankly. She swallowed the lump that had somehow found its way into her throat. "Nikolai, I—"

Whatever she was going to say was interrupted by the shrill ring of her doorbell. A timely interruption, she decided. With her emotions as scattered as they were, there was absolutely no telling what she might have blurted out to him if given the chance.

Saved by the bell.

That's what she thought, at least, until she saw who was on the other side of the peephole in her front door.

Chapter Eight

Miles.

Oh, Jesus, this was going to be awkward.

"It's OK," she told Nikolai, who'd stayed glued to her side all the way to the door. "It's my *friend*, Miles."

A muscle in Nikolai's jaw jumped, but other than that, his expression gave away nothing. She envied that about him. She'd bet he was one hell of an awesome poker player.

Violet took a deep breath and opened the door. "Miles, how nice to see you."

She let out a surprised squeak when Miles grabbed her and pulled her into a lung-squishing hug. Out of the corner of her eye, she saw Nikolai's body tense up as he took a warning step in her direction. She gave him a small shake of her head, and although his frown was grim as death, he crossed his arms over his chest and stayed put.

"Oh, my darling Violet," Miles said into her hair. "I was so worried about you. Are you alright?"

OK, first of all, the hug was weird. Miles had never been the touchy-feely type, nor was she. They'd been on a handful of dates and hadn't really progressed past a polite goodnight peck on the cheek.

And second of all…*my darling Violet?* Since when was an actuary so full of purple prose? She suddenly felt like the heroine in an '80s bodice-ripper with Fabio on the cover.

Not that there was really anything wrong with those. She'd certainly read more than her fair share of them back in the day. In fact—

Violet gave herself a sharp mental slap across the face. *Focus, damn it!*

Carefully extracting herself from his overly exuberant embrace, Violet stepped back and offered him what she hoped was a warm smile. "Of course I'm alright, Miles. Why wouldn't I be?"

Miles pushed his horn-rimmed glasses up with his index finger and fixed her with a stern look. "I heard about the break-in on my police scanner. You should have called me immediately."

Was it a bad sign for their relationship that calling him had never once entered her mind? Probably. "I'm sorry, Miles. I should've let you know what was going on. But I'm perfectly fine. My friend Harper has the entire investigation under control."

Miles's nose wrinkled up at the mention of Harper. They'd met once, and Violet had gotten the distinct impression that neither party had been impressed by the other. "Well," he said, "I'd feel more comfortable if you'd allow *me* to help with the investigation. After all, I'm sure your *friend* isn't aware that 59.6% of burglaries of single females are committed by someone the victim knows. I could definitely help define the suspect list."

A rough noise that sounded distinctly like a snort came from Nikolai, drawing Miles's attention to him for the first time. Miles's brows scrunched down in confusion as his gaze moved between Violet and Nikolai. "What's going on, Violet? Who's this?"

Violet wasn't entirely sure she appreciated his tone. He sounded decidedly judge-y that she was with another man. Going on a few dates didn't equal monogamy. She'd certainly never misled Miles in any way.

But now wasn't the time to argue that point, Violet decided. Not with Nikolai standing there, all tall and dark and brooding, glaring daggers at Miles.

"Miles," Violet said, "this is Nikolai Aleyev. He's working for Harper at the moment. He's the—" *Man who kidnapped me that one time? Embodiment of a walking wet dream? Guy who says he'd do anything for me and turns my knees to jelly?* "—bodyguard Harper hired to stay with me until the case is closed."

Again with the nose wrinkle. This time, Miles kind of looked like he'd just sniffed sour milk as his gaze moved over Nikolai. Nikolai kept his expression carefully blank, but there was a slight curl to his upper lip that could only be called a sneer of derision as he regarded Miles in return.

And suddenly Violet had a lot more empathy for her client, Mrs. Richards. The testosterone in the room was so thick you could practically slice it, plate it, and serve it with coffee. It was entirely possible that one or both of these guys was going to whip out his dick and pee on her at any moment to mark her as his territory.

Miles was the first to make a move. He stepped forward and stuck his hand out in Nikolai's direction, a challenging glint in his eyes. "Pleased to meet you."

There was nothing sincere in his words, and the look in his eyes made Violet nervous. Surely Miles wouldn't try the old finger-crushing handshake that men so enjoyed on Nikolai, would he? Violet cringed at the thought.

Nikolai stared at Miles's hand for a moment before taking it. When he did, she saw Miles's grip tighten to the point that his face actually showed the strain. Yep, Violet thought. Definitely the finger-crushing dude handshake.

Nikolai leaned forward ever so slightly, bared his teeth in a feral mockery of a smile, and muttered a greeting, but the growly tone of his voice made the pleasant words ring out like a threat. The corded muscles in his forearms flexed and pulled as Nikolai tightened his grip on Miles's hand.

Since it was entirely possible for a *dhampyre* to crush a normal human's bones with one well-executed squeeze, Violet knew Nikolai had probably backed the handshake off to less than half strength. But even that was enough to make Miles's face go white and a bead of sweat to break out on his upper lip.

Violet aimed a sharp glare at Nikolai until he let go of Miles's hand. The shrug and subtle smirk he offered her in return was completely unrepentant.

Ugh. Men.

Another moment of tense male staredown ensued, until Miles finally visually dismissed Nikolai and turned his attention back to Violet. He took hold of her shoulders and fixed her with a look so intense she was startled. She'd never seen Miles *do* intense.

"Violet," Miles said, "I think you should come stay with me until this is all over. I live in a gated community just outside of town. Crime rates are 47% higher outside of gated communities, as I'm sure you know."

No, she hadn't known that. Nor had she ever really cared. She was starting to see Lexa's point about all the stats Miles spewed. It really *was* kind of annoying. How had she not noticed that before?

He added, "I would be honored to protect you, my dear."

This time Nikolai's snort wasn't so subtle. "Violet stays here. She stays with me."

And while she agreed with Nikolai's statement, the note of possession behind his words didn't sit well with her inner feminist.

She narrowed her eyes on him. "Well, actually, *Violet* goes wherever *she* wants, since *she* is in charge of *herself* and *her* own destiny."

Miles shot Nikolai a quick look of smug triumph that Violet squashed by adding, "But Nikolai is right, Miles. I'm *choosing* to stay in my own home, and I *choose* to keep Nikolai in charge of my protection and Harper in charge of my case. But I really do thank you for your concern. It's very—" *Over the top? Strangely confident for an actuary? Clingy? Super freakin' weird?* "—flattering."

The frown he gave her reminded her of the look her mother used to give her when she was five and got caught with her hand in the Oreo jar. "Violet, dear, being safe isn't about…" he trailed off, giving Nikolai the sour-milk-sniffing look again, "…*brawn*. You don't always need a big, strong Neanderthal to protect you. Brains are even more important."

Wow, she thought, score another point for Lexa. Miles could *definitely* be a condescending jerk. He'd only uttered a few sentences, and in that short time, he'd managed to insult both her intelligence and Nikolai's.

Violet's "big, strong Neanderthal" shot her look that all but *begged* her to let him toss Miles out on his condescending ass. She grudgingly respected his restraint. He easily could've Hulk-ed out and acted like the muscle-bound thug Miles clearly thought he was. But so far, he'd maintained his composure, even if it was a somewhat *tense* composure.

In contrast, Miles looked on the verge of having an aneurysm. His usually pasty complexion had taken on a ruddy glow, and his posture was so rigid Violet wondered if he was trying to appear taller than he actually was.

Violet almost didn't blame him for that. Standing next to a guy who looked like Nikolai couldn't be easy for a guy who looked like Miles. To Miles, Nikolai—who probably had six inches on him in height and at least 20 pounds more lean muscle on his frame—probably looked like every bully who'd ever stuffed him into a locker in middle school.

Violet could relate. She'd certainly taken her fair share of bullying from the pretty people when she was the glasses-and-headgear-wearing president of the AV club in the ninth grade.

Yeah. Good times.

But just because she could relate to Miles's situation didn't mean she was going to tolerate his possessive behavior. She just had *way* too much going on in her world at the moment to deal with babying a delicate male ego. It was time to end this…whatever it was that she'd been having with Miles. Time to turn *Mr. Right Now* into *Mr. Yeah, Not So Much*.

Just not in front of Nikolai.

"I really do appreciate your concern, Miles," she said in what Lucas had always referred to as her talking-to-a-deranged-lunatic voice. "I'm comfortable and safe where I am, though." Carefully ignoring the fact that he was now so clearly vexed his skin was purple—*Jesus, that couldn't be healthy, could it?*—Violet asked, "Are we still on for drinks at Clary's tonight?"

Clary's Pub was the perfect place to dump someone. It wasn't *too* loud, but there was enough noise that no one would overhear if their conversation got heated in any way. And the ambiance was in no way intimate, which was exactly what she needed to put her relationship with Miles out of its misery.

"Yes, of course," Miles bit off.

After a too-wet and all kinds of awkward near-miss kiss (she managed to turn her mouth away just in the nick of time, thank God), Miles was on his way.

When he was gone, she closed the door, leaned her back against it, shut her eyes, and let out a sigh of relief. After tonight, she'd have one less source of stress in her life. Maybe she'd just give up on men after all. Lately they all just seemed to be more trouble than they were worth.

That's when her nipples went on high alert and she realized Nikolai had leaned against the door right next to her. His hand brushed hers and an annoying zing of electricity shot up her arm.

Ugh. Apparently her body just wasn't going to get onboard with her penis embargo anytime soon.

Stupid self-destructive body.

"So," he said, that deep voice and accent once again playing merry hell with her pulse and concentration, "we're going for drinks tonight?"

Violet blinked up at him. She'd totally forgotten that for the time being, anywhere she went, Nikolai went.

Which meant she was going to break up with Miles in front of Nikolai after all. He'd probably think her decision to end things with Miles had something to do with him, too.

And as he stood next to her, looking all tall, dark, and dangerous, turning her on and irritating her in equal measure, (Did anyone *really* have the right to be so damned sexy? It was gratuitous, really) she couldn't help but wonder if Nikolai would be *right* to think her breakup with Miles meant she was interested in dating him again.

Fuuuccckkk.

Tipping her gaze heavenward, she wondered what she'd done lately to piss *Him* off.

"I'm sure *He* has bigger concerns than your love life, *kotehok*," Nikolai answered with a smirk.

She closed her eyes again. "I said that out loud, didn't I?"

"Yes."

"Oh…balls."

He chuckled in a low, rough rumble that could only be described as panty-dropping.

It was going to be a long night. Again.

Chapter Nine

Nikolai had been waterboarded once as part of his Sentry reprogramming. It was the closest he'd ever come to breaking, to offering them whatever they wanted—to kill whomever they wanted him to kill—just to end the torture, the crippling, lung-seizing pain.

But right now? He'd almost rather be waterboarded than sit in this pub and watch the woman he wanted more than his next breath date another man.

There were so many things that were just *wrong* about this situation. First of all, there was the dress Violet had chosen for her night out.

It shouldn't have bothered him. The length was fine (just below the knee), and the neckline wasn't too low (it hit just below her collarbone), but it clung to her curves like it'd been designed just for her body (or with the sole purpose of driving him crazy). The fact that she'd put it on for anyone other than him made him want to punch something.

Preferably Miles's smug face.

Nikolai suppressed a growl at the thought of his conversation with the pretentious little prick earlier.

Miles was the other thing that was wrong with this situation. What was someone like Violet—smart, beautiful, kind, unassuming—doing with such a miserable excuse for a human being? At Violet's house, it'd been all he could do to keep from running the fucker's head through the wall. Fear of damaging Violet's home was pretty much all that had stopped him from doing just that.

"You know, instead of sitting here growling and brooding, you could just go over there and tell her how you feel," Harper said mildly.

And that was yet another problem with this evening. The company he'd been forced to keep.

Somehow, Harper had managed to find out that Violet had a date Nikolai would be forced to attend, and she thought it would be a "total hoot" (her words) to show up at the same bar and observe. And if that wasn't bad enough, she'd brought nearly her entire entourage along for the ride.

So far there was nothing…*hoot-y* about it.

Not. Any. Of. It.

Without taking his eyes off Violet, he said as dryly as he could manage, "I should go over there and tell her I'd like to string her date up from the rafters by his own entrails?"

Harper waited a beat before replying, "You might want to massage the verbiage on that a bit."

Beside her, Benny snickered and pantomimed a massage with his hands. Harper chuckled before bumping knuckles with him.

Nikolai held in a put-upon sigh as Seven said, "Maybe you should say it *exactly* like that. I don't like this guy. Scaring him off would be doing Violet a favor."

Nikolai glanced over at her, eyes narrowed. "Why? Do you know something about him?"

"No. It's just a feeling."

From his position standing behind Harper, arms crossed over his chest, Riddick added, "I don't like him, either, but his history's clean. He has no ties to the paranormal world. The chances of him being her stalker are next to nothing. And we know the guy who broke into her apartment was a vamp. This guy's about as mundane as he can get."

"There's still something about him that doesn't sit right with me," Seven insisted. "I'm going to talk to Lucas when he gets home tonight. Maybe the police can come up with something on him that we couldn't."

Riddick shrugged. "It's possible. I just don't see this guy as the violent or dangerous type, though. He's too soft looking."

Nikolai agreed. He still hated the guy. The mere fact that he'd been able to convince Violet to ever go out with him in the first place was reason enough for Nikolai to hate Miles. Then he saw Miles reach out across the table and cover Violet's hand with his own.

And *that* was the most powerful reason of all for Nikolai to hate Miles. *He* was allowed to touch her.

"You're growling again, Comrade," Harper sing-songed. He turned his growl on her, but she merely laughed and added, "Don't be so snarly. There's nothing to be jealous about. She's totally breaking up with him right now."

His gaze shot to Harper's. "How do you know this?"

"Body language. See how she's leaning away from him, talking calmly? And see how he's leaning in, looking more and more desperate with every word she says?"

He shifted his eyes back to Violet and saw her subtly slide her hand out from under Miles's and scoot her chair back ever so slightly. She was distancing herself from him physically, which made Nikolai want to disembowel Miles a little bit less. But only a little bit.

"And," Harper added, "the guy's a complete twatwaffle. There's no way someone like Violet would keep going out with a turd like him. He was most likely just a wedding date to her. And now that she's going with you, she doesn't need him anymore."

Nikolai didn't really have anything to contribute to that sentiment. He had no earthly idea what a *twatwaffle* was. His English was perfect, but some American colloquialisms were damn near impossible for foreigners like him to discern. And Harper was positively *brimming* with American colloquialisms.

"She's totally into you anyway, dude," Benny added. "I don't know what you're freaking out about. Whenever you aren't looking at her, she's looking at you."

Nikolai glanced back at Violet, only to see her immediately glance away. She *had* been looking at him!

Very interesting.

But even if she was attracted to him physically, how could she ever forgive him for everything he'd done to her? How could she ever trust him with her heart, as she agreed to trust him with her body for this assignment?

Harper laid a hand on his bicep. "Violet has the biggest heart of anyone I've ever known. She'll forgive you."

He'd be the luckiest bastard who ever lived if Harper was right.

Benny snorted. "Shit yeah, she will. You wouldn't believe some of the shit I've gotten Angela to forgive me for. What you did to Vi is tame in comparison, I guarantee you that."

He had no idea who Angela was, but something told Nikolai that asking Benny any questions on this particular topic would be ill-advised, so he kept his mouth shut.

Benny, however, had no such compunction.

"The whole midget porn thing, for example," Benny went on. "That was *huge*. And it took a lot of groveling on my part, but eventually, Angela was willing to pretend the whole thing never happened. All's well that ends well, you know?"

Harper opened her mouth, but snapped it shut when Riddick put a hand on her shoulder. She looked up at him, and he shook his head. "I beg you," Riddick said, a pained expression on his face. "If you love me even just a little bit, don't ask."

Harper sighed in defeat and looked back over at Benny. Nikolai could tell she was dying to ask more questions, but instead, she opted to say, "Pretty sure the term you want to use these days is 'little people,' Benny."

Benny sniffed. "Pfffttt. I can never keep that PC bullshit straight. Swear to God it changes every damn day. You can't say nothin' no more without offending some special little snowflake, you know?"

Violet stood up and starting moving toward the ladies' room. *Thank you, Jesus.* Nikolai now had an excuse to get the hell out of Benny and Harper's conversation.

He kept his eyes on Violet, but his peripheral vision was solid enough that he saw Miles throw his napkin to the table in a fit of temper and storm out the door.

Good riddance, he thought. One reason for Violet to push Nikolai away was now out of the picture. Now he only had about, oh, maybe a thousand or so others to overcome.

"You're so screwed, Aleyev," he muttered.

Behind him, Benny cackled and piped up with, "Yeah, and not even in the fun way!"

Chapter Ten

Violet was on the verge of a complete emotional breakdown.

Her conversation with Miles was so draining she could barely hold her head up anymore. Leaning heavily on the sink in the ladies' room, she sucked in a few deep breaths and blotted some shiny spots on her forehead with a tissue.

Miles had argued with her so much about breaking up that she'd actually broken a sweat while she debated it with him. What the hell was the world coming to when the classic "it's not you, it's me" speech didn't send a member of the opposite sex running for the door?

But the arguing and Miles's assertions that they were soulmates and would eventually end up together (after all, did she know that 58% of second-chance romances ended in happy marriages?) weren't what bothered Violet most. When Miles had asked her if her decision to break up with him was because of Nikolai, she'd opened her mouth to say it didn't, and…nothing came out.

Violet had no doubt she would've eventually broken up with Miles. They mostly got along fine, sure, but there weren't any *sparks*. No zing. She would've needed some *zing* sooner or later.

But as Nikolai sat there, two tables away, looking at her with more intensity and zing than Miles would ever be capable of, Violet couldn't lie and say the break-up's timing didn't have at least a *little* something to do with Nikolai.

And didn't that just make her a hundred different kinds of fool?

She was starting to feel like she was being ripped apart, caught in the middle of a war between her body, her heart, and her brain. Her body, of course, wanted her to jump Nikolai at the first opportunity and bend him to her will. (Or let him bend her to *his* will, preferably right over the edge of her bed.)

Her heart was only slightly more cautious than her body. Her brain, her last line of defense, knew that getting involved with Nikolai again was a dangerous proposition at best.

All her life she'd led with her head and protected her heart. Until she met Nikolai, that is. And where did trusting her heart get her? Kidnapped and tied to a chair, that's where.

Violet took a deep breath and checked herself out in the mirror. Overly bright eyes stared back at her. Her cheeks were flushed, too. Chest rising and falling with rapid breaths. She was either seconds away from a panic attack, or in the throes of rampant sexual frustration. At this point it was hard to determine which.

She had to get her shit together, and soon. There was only so much more of this *angst* she could take in her life. Violet Marchand was the person you *went* to for help with your problems, not the person who could *commiserate* with you about your problems because she had so damn many of her own.

"Pull yourself together, woman. You're losing your damn mind," she muttered to her reflection before grabbing her bag and swinging the door open.

And right there, waiting for her, leaning back against the wall opposite the ladies' room, stood the object of her internal war. He pushed away from the wall when he saw her.

And that's when she lost what little grip on her emotions she had left.

She held up a hand to ward him off. "Please, don't, Nikolai. I'm in the middle of an existential crisis and I can't have you looking like—" she gestured to his face and body "—*that* around me right now."

He frowned and glanced down at himself, obviously trying to see what was wrong with the way he looked and what had her so twisted in knots. And *that* twisted her up even more, because there was absolutely *nothing* wrong with the way he looked. Now he was probably thinking he had parsley struck between his front teeth, given the disgusted way she was glaring at him. He had no way of knowing it was his unholy level of hotness that was wrecking her sanity.

But she was *way* too far gone down the rat hole of her

breakdown to clearly articulate *that*, so with a disgusted, inarticulate groan, she threw up her hands and walked past him. She'd just made it out the front door of the pub when he grabbed her hand.

"Violet." Although she stubbornly kept her gaze trained on her car—her last hope of escaping Nikolai's clutches with her dignity intact—in the parking lot, she let him pull her to a stop. "Violet, look at me."

Ugh. That was the *last* thing she should do. If she *looked* at him, her brain would melt and she wouldn't be able to think.

His fingers tightened around hers, making her realize she was stuck. He wouldn't let go until she met his eyes.

You can do this, her brain encouraged. *You're smart and strong.*

Locking her jaw, she turned around. Her eyes moved up over his narrow waist, solid chest, broad shoulders, his square jaw, and locked on his gaze.

"Why do you run from me, *kotehok*?" he asked, his accent a little thicker than usual, his voice sounding completely earnest. "You can trust me. I swear it."

She swallowed hard, unable to look away. She *shouldn't* trust him. Trusting him was *terrifying*. Like deep sea diving with only a half tank of oxygen in shark-infested waters. Like free-falling out of a plane without checking to see if she'd even packed a parachute.

But God help her, she had so few defenses against the absolute sincerity she heard in his voice.

He tugged her closer, and her body—the traitorous slut—gave in without a fight. "Let me help you."

The rasp of his voice, the way his warm breath brushed her ear as he spoke, the heat she felt rolling off his skin…it was all so *tempting*. All she had to do was lean in closer and sink into that heat and take that strength for her own. For once, she wouldn't have to be the strong one.

Then his words hit her.

Clenching her teeth, she took a step back. "*You* can't help me!" she bit out in frustration. "*You're* the cause of my breakdown! How *dare* you stand there—all tall and muscly and crazy hot—and have *absolutely* no clue that you're driving me insane!"

His brow furrowed as he processed her ramblings, and after a long moment, one corner of his mouth tipped up in a hint of a self-satisfied smirk. "You think I'm crazy hot?"

She threw her hands up. "Everything I just said and *that* was your takeaway?"

"Um…yes?"

She glared at him as her desire and anxiety and irritation swirled together in a lava-like cocktail that seemed to be burning its way through her bloodstream. It was official. She didn't need to worry about the death threats because her bodyguard was going to be the death of her. "You are just so…so…"

"So…what, *kotehok*?" His eyes dropped to her mouth. "Crazy hot?" There was a lilt of humor in his voice she didn't appreciate at all.

Not. At. All.

A sound that was something like the love child of a shriek and a groan tore from her throat and she started to turn away, fully prepared to flounce—an honest-to-God, full-on Scarlett-O'Hara-level *flounce*—to her car. But his fingers closed around her wrist, tugging her back to him.

Violet opened her mouth to tell him to back off, but then her gaze clashed with his. All traces of humor and amusement at her expense were gone. The heat and hunger in his eyes made her snap her mouth shut and rooted her in place.

Then his lips were on hers and Violet's brain gave up the fight.

OK, body and heart. Looks like you win this round.

Chapter Eleven

The first time Violet had kissed Nikolai, he'd been shocked. There'd been an agonizing minute of hesitation on his part that haunted her to this day. She hadn't even been sure he was going to kiss her back. It'd been utterly *mortifying*.

But there was no hesitation this time.

It wasn't a movie-perfect kiss. There was way too much urgency in it for that. But all of the worry and frustration she'd been wallowing in all day melted away under a tidal wave of raw, pure *need*.

Violet had never been the focus of the kind of intensity Nikolai brought to their kiss. He seemed to be pouring everything he had into driving her out of her mind with want just in case he never got another opportunity to kiss her.

But Violet wasn't about to let him have *all* the control, either. She gave as good as she got, going so far as to snag his lower lip between her teeth.

With a growl that bordered on feral, Nikolai slid a hand behind her head and tilted her face a bit so he could deepen their kiss. On and on it went—and it was *wonderful*.

He yanked her up against him when her knees threatened to give out, and she would've been grateful for the save if she hadn't been too turned on to think straight.

Violet couldn't remember ever feeling anything like *this*.

She couldn't touch enough of him at once. Her hands slid greedily up his arms, over his shoulders, up through his hair, and back down again.

Nikolai seemed to be having the same problem when it came to touching her. His hands moved over her like it was his job to make her come with nothing more than his mouth on hers and his hands on her body.

And he apparently *loved* his job.

She let out a shocked gasp, quickly followed by a long, embarrassing groan of pleasure, when he grabbed her hips and pulled her into his body so tightly she felt the hard evidence of just *how much* he loved his job pressed into her stomach.

The wave of need that hit her was so unexpected she fell into him, knocking them off-balance. Nikolai braced his legs to catch them both, all the while never losing his grip on her. He did it so easily, as if she weighed nothing at all.

And that *so* wasn't the case.

He broke their kiss to whisper something in Russian in her ear. There was so much gravel in his voice that the words barely sounded human. A shiver ran through her from head to toe. She had no idea what he'd said, but at that moment, it didn't matter. Whatever he'd asked her for, he could have it.

"Yes," she whispered back. "Please."

He pulled back to look down into her eyes, and the stark, desperate need and desire she'd read in his expression earlier slowly started morphing into something softer and infinitely more dangerous. He brushed his fingertips, feather-soft, over her lips, his eyes moving over her like he was trying to memorize the lines of her face. "*Kotehok*, I—"

Whatever he was going to say was swallowed up by what sounded like a car backfiring, the sound so loud and so close it threatened to burst her eardrums. A piece of the brick wall behind them shattered and flew up, slicing across her cheekbone.

Before she could catch her breath or figure out what was going on, Nikolai yanked her around the corner of the building. He shoved her against the brick and pinned her there with his body, holding her head against his chest. His heart thundered under her ringing ears.

"What the hell's going on?" she asked, unable to keep a shrill note of panic out of her voice.

"Someone shot at us," he said.

He didn't sound like himself, she thought. The tender, passionate man who'd kissed the hell out of her a moment ago had been body snatched by someone else entirely—someone harder, colder.

Violet's stomach lurched. A bullet had torn into the brick wall *right by their heads* while they'd been kissing. If they'd moved so much as an inch to the right, one or both of them would be dead.

And it was her fault.

She couldn't even tell if it was terror or guilt and regret clogging her throat at the moment. Nikolai was literally shielding her with his body so that if any more shots were fired, he'd take the bullet instead of her.

She'd logically known that was the job he'd signed on for, and he'd said he'd be willing to take a bullet for her. But *saying* it and actually *doing* it were two entirely different things. And up until this moment, shivering against a brick wall in an alley, every muscle in her body clenching in anticipation of the next gunshot, she hadn't *really* believed she was in any *real* danger.

She knew differently now.

Violet was about to apologize to him when she was interrupted by the sound of police sirens. They got louder and louder, then went silent.

She lifted her chin to glance up at Nikolai. "Do you think the shooter is gone?" she asked.

He didn't answer right away, just stared down at her, scowling fiercely at the cut on her cheek. She brushed her fingers over it and they came away smeared with blood. Maybe it was the rush of adrenaline caused by the fear of dying—and if she was being totally honest, Nikolai's kiss before the shot was fired—but the slice barely hurt. "It's nothing," she told him. "I'm fine."

His frown didn't lessen, but he said, "Whoever took the shot is gone. Someone inside must have called the police right away, because it sounds like they're on the scene already."

She opened her mouth again to apologize, and this time it wasn't sirens that interrupted her.

"Why the hell are people always shooting at my friends?" a very disgruntled Harper demanded, stomping around the corner with Riddick in tow. "It's *really* starting to piss me off!"

"Tell me someone saw the shooter," Nikolai growled.

"Benny's talking to a couple of people who were across the street when the shot was fired," Riddick said, "but you two were the only ones out in front of the pub." He shot a disgusted look up toward a street lamp with a busted-out bulb. "And it's dark as shit out here. We might get lucky and find someone who got a make and model of the getaway car, but I can't imagine anyone caught a glimpse of the guy, or even a partial plate. I'm not too hopeful at this point."

Harper snorted. "Are you ever?"

He shot her a disgruntled look. "Sometimes. But mostly, people are completely unobservant and just generally useless."

She rolled her eyes and smirked at her husband. "That's inspiring. We should have it stitched on throw pillows for our living room. You always know—"

"This isn't a fucking joke," Nikolai interrupted, his tone sharp enough to make Violet flinch.

"I warned you about using that tone with my wife, asshole," Riddick snarled.

Violet was still two-fisting Nikolai's shirt and had her head practically buried in his chest, but she still felt his body tense, preparing to dive into whatever battle Riddick wanted to wage.

"Whoa," Harper said, stepping forward and holding a hand up to each of the hulking *dhampyres* who looked like they wanted to tear each other apart. "Let's just chill out, OK? Fighting each other isn't going to get us anywhere. Nikolai, stay with Violet while the police take your statements, then get her home. Riddick, Benny, and I will take it from there." Harper shot Violet a small smile. "You've got nothing to worry about, OK, doc? We've got you covered."

Violet swallowed hard while her relief and guilt battled it out for top billing of her emotional state. Everyone having her *covered* was exactly what was worrying her the most.

Because it was now 100% clear that anyone covering her was also standing right in front of a bullet.

Chapter Twelve

Nikolai struggled with a great many things during his time with Sentry. He struggled with following orders without question. He fought against policy and procedure that made no sense to him. He questioned if what he was doing for Sentry was right or wrong. The one thing he'd never struggled with was his focus.

Until now.

He'd been so damned focused on Violet—the feel of her body against his, the sweet taste of her on his tongue, the tidal wave of need and want he could feel flowing between them—that he hadn't noticed the presence of a threat until a shot had been fired.

He could've gotten her killed.

Nikolai had experienced his fair share of guilt over the years, but the guilt he felt at having let Violet down was an entirely different animal. Had he not been so wrapped up in her, maybe he would've noticed the threat sooner, gotten her to safety faster.

He should've let her keep him at arm's length. It was clearly what she wanted. But he just hadn't been able to leave her alone. His heart had hurt at the mere thought of it.

Nikolai was pulled out of his solitary pity party by Violet's deep sigh as she sank down on the sofa. "I didn't think we were *ever* going to get out of that police station."

He sat next to her and rested his elbows on his splayed knees, choosing to remain silent. Violet was being facetious, but in the interrogation room where he'd given his statement with Violet, Nikolai had seriously wondered if the police really *would* let him leave. They'd had so many questions for Violet about what she was doing with Nikolai that it didn't take a genius to figure out they suspected him. Maybe he wasn't a suspect in the shooting, but they clearly thought something he was involved in was creating problems for Violet.

The detective who'd been assigned to the case had even asked him questions about his time with Sentry and what he'd done for them. He'd asked Nikolai why some former Sentry cleaners were referred to as White Death.

It had taken every ounce of restraint—restraint that was already stretched to its limits by the night's events—to keep from knocking the detective's teeth down his throat until he choked on them. But Nikolai was certain his Council-appointed PO would frown upon him assaulting police officers, so he'd taken several deep, even breaths before calmly explaining to the small-minded motherfucker exactly what he wanted to know.

Nikolai Aleyev was White Death personified.

Not every Sentry cleaner was qualified to be White Death, which went way beyond simple target elimination and getting rid of evidence. White Death was a fancy name for someone who erased a person's entire identity, getting rid of everyone they'd ever known, loved, or even met casually. It took years sometimes to complete such an assignment, and could cost hundreds of innocents their lives.

Nikolai had been White Death for more than a few vampires in his time with Sentry. Not even Seven knew that about him.

He'd been White Death for his last assignment with Sentry before its shutdown. He'd wiped out every person who'd ever come in contact with his target except for one.

Because that *one* happened to be a seven-year-old boy who'd watched Nikolai's vampire target murder his mother.

Nikolai would never forget the look on that child's face when White Death came for him. The boy was so young, yet he'd seen so much darkness in his life that having a gun pointed at him hadn't even scared him. He'd looked resigned. As if he'd known his life couldn't have ended any other way.

Nikolai knew that feeling. He'd seen that same resigned look staring back at him in the mirror.

Killing the boy wasn't an option at that point. Instead, he did the only thing he was good at other than killing.

He made the boy disappear.

New family, new identity, new country…not even the most powerful, covert agencies in the world could find that boy now.

His efforts had earned him a three-week stint in reprogramming. They used sleep and sensory deprivation that time, if he remembered correctly. He'd done so much time in reprogramming with so many different methods of torture that sometimes he forgot which stint was which and what he'd done—or refused to do—to earn his time there.

But that didn't matter now. His past, the torture, the death and destruction that followed him through his life like his own personal storm cloud…it wasn't important. He'd go through reprogramming a thousand times over if it helped keep Violet safe.

She'd been amazing during their time at the police station. Indignation on his behalf stiffened her spine as she sat in that interrogation room. She'd accused the detective of leading a witch hunt, and demanded to speak to the man's commanding officer. When that demand was refused, she'd promised to have the man's badge once she lodged a formal complaint with the Vampire Council on Nikolai's behalf. She'd been fierce, warrior-like in her defense of his integrity.

It had been a huge turn-on while at the same time, succeeded in gouging the knife of guilt into his heart just a little deeper.

He didn't deserve to have a woman like Violet defend him.

Violet surprised him out of his brooding by reaching over and grabbing his hand. "That detective had no right to say those things to you," she said quietly.

As if to further prove he had no control when it came to Violet, his hand turned over and he laced his fingers through hers. Her hand was so small in his, her long, slim fingers pale against his much thicker, inelegant ones. "It was all true," he said, wondering how long it would be before she pulled away from him. She should. He certainly wouldn't blame her for it.

Even if it would kill him just a little more inside.

But she didn't pull away. Instead, her fingers tightened around his. She cleared her throat. "You know, when I told you the past was done and we could move forward—that I was over everything that happened between us? Well, I was lying. I wasn't at all ready to forgive you for what you did to me."

Yep, he thought, there it was. The knife in the heart. It was every bit as painful as what he'd expected.

"But," she went on, "after what you did for me tonight, how could I not forgive you, Nikolai?" She shook her head and raised her eyes to his. "I forgive you," she whispered. "I'd like for us to start over."

For a fraction of a second, his chest swelled with hope at her words. Maybe this...*whatever* it was between them had a chance after all. If *she* could forgive him, surely he could learn to forgive himself. Right?

Then reality settled in, as it always did, leaving the bloody corpse of hope in its wake. "Thank you, *kotebok*. You have no idea what that means to me," he said, his voice gruff with emotion. "But you were right to refuse me. At least until this is all over. If what happened tonight isn't proof of that, than I don't know what is. I can't protect you if I'm…"

Kissing you. Touching you. Wanting you more than I need my next breath. Falling hopelessly in love with you a little bit more every day.

"…dating you," he finished lamely.

She could never play poker, his Violet. Every emotion she was feeling in that moment was written plainly all over her lovely face. Disappointment, embarrassment, a little hint of irritation…it was all there as she pulled her hand away from his and averted her eyes. "I understand. And I'm sure you're right. It will be best to keep our relationship professional."

His finger, which apparently still had a mind of its own, ran lightly along her jaw, applying just enough pressure that she had to look up at him again. "You have to know that's not what I want. But I'm trying to do the right thing for once in my life. I need to keep you safe, and this is the only way I know how to do it."

She swallowed hard and nodded. "I understand. Maybe we can be friends until this whole thing is over?"

Can you be friends with someone you want more than your next breath? It seemed unlikely. But what choice did he have? "Of course, *kotehok*."

She tentatively took his hand again and they both did their level best to ignore the zing of electricity that flowed between them. That *always* flowed between them.

Friends, Nikolai thought bitterly. Sure. What could possibly go wrong?

Chapter Thirteen

Is it normal to notice how good your "friend" smells? Or how gentle his big hands can be as they clean and bandage a cut on your cheek? Or how the looks he gives you when he thinks you aren't looking are powerful enough to melt the clothes right off your body?

Well, Violet was sort of an expert on the human psychological condition, and she knew the answer to all of those questions was a great, big, fat, resounding *no*. And yet it was all crap she'd felt for Nikolai since he refused her clumsy attempt at saying she wanted another chance with him.

She understood where he was coming from. He couldn't focus on protecting her if he was focused on, well, doing anything personal—and naked—with her. Hadn't Kevin Costner said pretty much the same thing to Whitney Houston in *The Bodyguard*?

God, how she *hated* that movie.

But while she understood everything he'd said, the irony of it all was still a bit of a throat-punch. He'd been on her doorstep only a day ago, asking for a second chance with her and she'd refused him. Shut him down cold. And now, only a few hours later after he'd nearly melted all her brain cells with the hottest kiss the world had ever known, she agreed to give him a second chance, and *he* shut *her* down.

It was all so ironic she could practically hear Alanis

Morissette singing about it in her head as if that whole damn song was nothing but the story of Violet's life.

Violet rolled over and glanced at the glowing green numbers on her alarm clock. Ugh. 3:45am. She was going to look like an extra on *The Walking Dead* the next day. And not one of the cute human survivors you just knew was going to die at any minute, but one of the oozing, shuffling zombies that looked like it probably smelled like week-old roadkill.

She'd fallen asleep the minute her head hit the pillow after her talk with Nikolai, but she'd found that staying asleep was beyond her. Her dreams were a frantic mix of terrifying scenarios (like getting shot at or kidnapped) and sensual ones (like rolling around in tangled, sweaty sheets with Nikolai).

If she were to psychoanalyze her own dreams, she'd say the threat of possible death hanging over her head was causing her subconscious to create a life-affirming scenario. And there was nothing more life-affirming than the deeply emotional and physical act of joining with another person.

Or maybe she was just stressed out and horny because she hadn't had sex in over a year and she was trapped in her house with the hottest man alive—a man who refused to be anything more than her friend until he was no longer responsible for guarding her life.

But then again maybe she was just all fucked up in the head. Who knew? Psychology was a *terribly* complicated thing.

She groaned out loud and gave her pillow a good solid karate chop. It didn't help her fall back to sleep, but hitting something sure as hell felt good. She did it again. Yep, it really *did* feel good. Maybe she shouldn't always preach nonviolence to her patients. Maybe if they could just hit something every now and then, they could—

"What's wrong?" the object of her sexual frustration said from her doorway.

Violet lifted her head to glance up at him and had to choke back a gasp. Had she fallen asleep again? Was she stuck in another nightmare that was going to slowly morph into a wet dream? She blinked a few times to see if the vision before her would go away. It didn't.

Holy. Fuck.

Backlit by the buttery soft lamplight in the guestroom across the hall, Nikolai stood with his arms braced on the doorjamb. He was wearing a pair of beat-to-hell, low-slung jeans with the top button undone.

And…that was all.

She'd seen him once without his shirt, and the sight had pretty much shaved a quick 20 points off her IQ. And that had been on a public street in the harsh glare of early morning sunlight. But seeing him like this *now*, in the middle of the night, in her *bedroom* doorway?

Mind. Blown.

Was it even *possible* that he looked harder and leaner than ever before? Smooth tanned skin, narrow waist, broad chest and shoulders…holy crap, he looked like someone had spent hours airbrushing him in Photoshop.

"W-What?" she asked, silently damning herself for sounding so breathy, like some kind of second-rate porn star.

He must've thought she hadn't heard him, because he came into her room and eased himself down on the edge of the bed next to her. The shift and play of his muscles as he moved was damn near hypnotic.

"What's wrong?" he repeated. "Why can't you sleep?"

Because I'm thinking about counting your ab muscles with my tongue? Because I've been celibate for a freakin' year and you're walking around my house looking like the most awesome sex toy ever built? Because I was half in love with you when you kidnapped me and now that I've decided to forgive you I can't have you? Because if you got hurt—or worse—trying to protect me it would break me into so many pieces I'd never be able to fix myself?

"I, um, don't know."

He frowned and brushed his fingertip over the butterfly bandage on her cheek. She barely resisted the urge to lean into his touch and purr like a cat.

"Does it hurt?" he asked, his voice gruff. "Can I get you anything?"

Violet swallowed hard to dislodge the lump that had settled in her throat. He was trying to take care of her. No one had taken care of her since she was a kid.

And his kindness made her feel even guiltier. Both for putting him danger and for the way her imagination had been shamelessly using and abusing his perfect body all night.

"It doesn't hurt," she told him.

She opened her mouth again to tell him she didn't need anything, but snapped it shut when she realized it would be a lie. She absolutely needed something.

Too bad it was something he'd already said he could no longer offer her.

He tilted his head to the side. "You can tell me, you know. Whatever is bothering you? We can talk about it. Isn't that what…friends would do?"

Was it her imagination, or did his tone sour on the word "friends?" She sighed. Wishful thinking on her part, most likely. "I know you said I didn't owe you any thanks or gratitude, but I do. Ever since I was a kid, I was the one people came to when they had a problem. I've never been the one who needed help, you know?"

One corner of his mouth quirked up. "I can believe that about you."

Emotion tightened her throat again. "But…here you are, taking care of me, not expecting anything in return for it. And earlier? Shielding me like you did?" She shook her head. "No one's ever done anything like that for me before. I just…I can't thank you enough, Nikolai. It means so, so much to me."

He ran a hand over the back of his neck and broke eye contact to glance towards her bedroom window. It was too dark out there for him to actually see anything, but he kept looking, pensive.

Violet let him have his moment to contemplate whatever he was going to say next. She owed him at least that much. And while she waited, she found herself focusing on his arms, the way the muscles shifted under his tanned skin as his hands clenched and unclenched. He was clearly uncomfortable with her gratitude.

After a few more seconds, he let out a harsh breath and lowered his head. "I'm not exactly sure how to respond to that," he said quietly.

She ducked her own head so that he was forced into eye contact before offering him a crooked smile of her own. "Well, didn't you just get done telling me I can talk to you about whatever's bothering me because that's what friends would do? Same rules apply to you, you know."

His brow furrowed as he choose his words. "When I first came to Whispering Hope, I didn't know anything about you. All I knew was that Sentry wanted me and all the other cleaners dead. It was probably the only mission I never questioned, not even once. We'd all done such horrible things." He paused, clearing his throat.

Violet fought the urge to reach for him, to offer him comfort. Something about the ridged set of his shoulders told her the gesture wouldn't be appreciated at the moment. Instead, she clasped her hands tightly in her lap, just in case they suddenly got a mind of their own.

"When I first saw you with Seven," he went on, "I felt something I'd never felt before."

"What did you feel?" she prodded gently.

"Curiosity," he answered with a self-deprecating chuckle. His gaze slid over her face, his expression softening to something Violet could only describe as awe. "I was fascinated by you, which made no sense. You weren't my target. All I needed to know about you was whether or not you could help me complete my mission to neutralize Seven. But I wanted to know more about you."

"What did you want to know?"

"Everything," he answered without hesitation. "I wanted to know why the face you show the world is different than the one you show your friends and loved ones. Why you bring the homeless man who lives behind Harper's building Italian food from Dominic's every Tuesday, and why you sit and eat with him, talking like you're best friends in a 5-star restaurant instead of in a filthy alley next to a dumpster. Why you stop to look at the puppies in the pound every weekend but never take one home."

Oh, wow, Violet thought. She'd been aware that his stalking (surveillance…whatever) of Seven had led to more than a few instances of Nikolai watching Violet. She'd been appalled by the invasion of privacy, of course. But now it was all even more confusing. He noticed things through his camera lens that even her closest friends didn't know about her. It was like…he'd gotten to know her without ever having met her.

And was it wrong that the idea of him watching her and wanting to know more about her turned her on just a tiny little bit? Maybe she had to add exhibitionism to her list of issues that only seemed to pop up in Nikolai's presence.

His attention dropped to her lips as she licked them nervously. He leaned forward just enough for her to catch a whiff of the soap he'd used—hers—when he'd showered earlier. Funny how something as simple as Ivory soap could smell so damn edible on his skin when it smelled so uninspiring on her own.

"But more than anything," he went on, his voice lower, raspier than before, "I wanted to know why the most beautiful woman I'd ever seen in my life went home alone each night. And would there ever be a time when she might consider going home with me."

Violet's lungs seized up. She *had* considered going home with him. More than once, in fact. And here he was, half-naked in her bed, looking at her with eyes so hot and full of desire it was a little intimidating.

Men didn't normally look at her like *that*. Nikolai looked at her like if he had to choose between touching her and drawing breath, he'd happily die to be near her.

"There was a time," she whispered.

There is a time.

Her words seemed to hit him like a punch to the gut. He let out a deep breath and closed his eyes. "And then I ruined my chance with you." He shook his head. "If I had it all to do over again, I'd do everything differently. But at that time, I saw you with Seven and I panicked. The thought of her hurting you…" he paused, his Adam's apple bobbing as he swallowed hard, "…was unthinkable. I didn't understand why I felt that way or what I needed to do about it, but I knew for sure that the world was a better place with you in it. I couldn't let her—or anyone—hurt you."

He'd kidnapped her to keep her safe, she realized. She'd always kind of assumed that he'd kidnapped her to get to Seven. He'd let her assume that, too. Probably because he knew it would be easier for her to move on with her life after he was gone if she hated him.

Violet's mouth went dry. Her first instincts about him had been right all along. He *was* a good man, not at all the villain he clearly thought he was.

So...what the hell was she supposed to do with all this new information?

If she was talking to one of her patients, she'd say follow your heart. Ironically enough, Violet had never really managed to do that for herself.

Maybe it was time to change things up a bit.

Without allowing her brain any time to argue, she threw herself at him, wrapping her arms around his waist and pressing her cheek over his heart. He stiffened in her hold, his entire body going rigid. She just held on tighter.

After a moment, he gave in and wrapped his arms around her. With a sigh, he rested his cheek against the top of her head. The strength of his body and heat of his skin surrounded her, and for the first time in a *long* time, Violet truly felt safe, like everything was going to be fine.

"Thank you," she choked out past the lump of emotion that had settled in her throat.

"For what?"

"For agreeing to stay with me until this thing is over. For caring about what happens to me. For explaining why you did what you did so beautifully. For being *you*," she finished lamely.

He grunted. "You deserve so much more. Having you look at me like I'm a hero…it's the only thing I've wanted in a long, long time. But it's not real. You need to know that. I'm the farthest thing from a hero, *kotehok*."

"The past doesn't mean anything. Not anymore. Only today matters. And today, you're *my* hero."

If she was in a therapy session with a client, she'd say the moment she'd just shared with Nikolai was a breakthrough in their relationship. She lifted her head to tell him that, but the words stuck in her throat.

He was staring down at her with a look that went so far beyond lust it shocked her. This was *need*, pure and simple, raw and elemental. So beautiful.

It was in that moment Violet realized being friends with Nikolai would never work. Because as his pupils dilated, the black nearly swallowing up the green, and he pulled in a deep, slow breath, an answering need deep within her started blazing a path through her blood.

He cupped the back of her neck in his palm and leaned in to rest his forehead against hers. "Tell me to leave," he rasped, sounding desperate.

That was the one thing Violet *couldn't* do at the moment. She shook her head.

Nikolai muttered harshly under his breath. Violet didn't need to understand Russian to know he'd just spit out a string of curses. She tumbled forward onto her elbows when he practically jumped off the bed.

He turned back toward her, but stared at a point somewhere just over her shoulder. Shoving both hands through his hair, he said, "I can't do this. I *won't* do this. Not now. You could've *died* tonight. I can't take advantage of how you're feeling right now. It all might change when Harper finds the shooter and you're out of danger. Hell, it all might change tomorrow after you think back on everything you heard about me today."

Her poor brain was confused for a moment as it tried to do the math on why Nikolai wasn't kissing her, why he was so far away. She'd always sucked at math.

But as she replayed his words, Violet's lust started melting into something infinitely warmer and more dangerous. As if safeguarding her body wasn't enough, Nikolai was now guarding her emotional state. He was afraid she'd regret being with him when there was no longer a death threat hanging over her head.

It was so *sweet*. Misguided and completely wrong, but *sweet*.

Violet remembered Harper telling her about how Riddick had tried to push her away for her own good once, too. But Harper hadn't let that stop her from getting what she wanted, and neither should Violet.

What would Harper do in this situation?

Well, Harper *damn* sure wouldn't make it easy for him to walk away. Of *that* Violet was certain.

Violet stared up at him with what she hoped was a complete lack of guile and said, "I understand. You're probably right."

A muscle in his jaw jumped as he gave her a terse nod. "Good night, Violet."

When he turned away from her and started moving toward the door, she asked, as casually as she could muster, "Would kissing me goodnight count as taking advantage of how I'm feeling?" She bit her lip. "Friends kiss friends goodnight sometimes, don't they?"

He stopped dead in his tracks. His fists opened and closed at his sides as a battle between what he *wanted* to do and what he thought was the *right* thing to do waged within him.

Inwardly, Violet smiled. Harper would be so proud of her.

But whatever smugness she'd earned quickly evaporated when Nikolai spun on his heel, stalked back to the bed, cupped her face in his hands and kissed the ever-loving crap out of her.

The look in his eyes when he raised his head was hot enough to make steam rise off her skin. "Good night, Violet."

He was gone before Violet could find her voice.

Chapter Fourteen

He was a fucking idiot.

The woman of his dreams had been in his arms—warm, grateful, *willing*—and he'd turned her away.

His dick would likely never forgive him.

It'd been about an hour since he'd said goodnight to her, and he'd been pacing from one end of her apartment to the other ever since. She'd fallen back to sleep immediately.

He was quickly finding that out about Violet—she could fall asleep faster than anyone he'd ever met. He wished he could say the same about himself. His years with Sentry had taught him to survive and function on little to no sleep for days on end, weeks if necessary. Now, even when he *wanted*, sleep it remained elusive.

Nikolai knew better than to even *try* to sleep tonight. Not after having been so close to Violet. The sweet, sultry scent of her skin, the silken feel of her arms as they tightened around his waist, the warmth of her breath as it skated across his chest, the honeyed taste of her…

Jesus. He paused in his pacing to adjust his jeans, which were quickly growing way too restrictive.

What the fuck had he been thinking when he got out of that bed? He'd been at the fucking gates of heaven, and he'd pretty much told Saint Peter, "No, thanks. I'd rather not come in. I'll just stay out here in hell all by myself."

"Fucking idiot," he muttered.

But even as he cursed himself, he'd realized something in that moment, in Violet's arms, that forced him to take a step back.

Everything about Violet just felt *right*. He couldn't think of one thing in his life that had felt right since he was a kid back in Russia all those years ago.

To him, Violet was home.

And it wasn't just the physical pull of her. It was much more. Like the way she blurted out her inner most thoughts when she was nervous. Like the way she took care of everyone around her before she even thought of taking care of herself. Like how she'd forgiven him for everything he'd done to her.

And she was so damn smart. Smarter than he could ever hope to be. She'd devoted her life to helping people, people who had no one else. That was his Violet. Champion of the hopeless lost causes. He loved that about her.

He loved…her.

Sentry had stripped nearly everything away from him, but they hadn't been able to touch the part of him that remembered what love was. It'd been so long since he'd felt it that it'd taken him a while to recognize it, but he'd been halfway in love with her when he kidnapped her all those months ago. Being with her today had just finished the job.

But it was *way* too soon to tell Violet how he felt. Not to mention it was the worst possible time in the world to dump *one more thing* on her. She was dealing with more than she should have to as it was.

What had given him the strength—or stupidity...however he wanted to look at it—to walk away from her tonight had been his complete obliviousness to how she felt about him. He knew she was attracted to him...but love? How could she possibly *love* him? She didn't know him nearly as well as he knew her.

She hadn't had the advantage of stalking him for weeks before they even met, after all.

So, the real question now was how the hell was he going to make her love him back? Because letting her go wasn't an option now. It wasn't fair to her, and he wasn't good enough for her by a long shot, but he was a selfish bastard. He'd be damned if he was going to lose the only woman who'd managed to make him feel *human* again.

Yes, the timing was terrible. That much was true. They had to figure out who was trying to kill her before he could focus on winning her heart for real. But that was alright with Nikolai. One of the only useful things Sentry had taught him was patience, and he had an abundance of it.

Their time would come. And speaking of time…

Glancing at the hints of sunlight that were starting to peep through Violet's heavy curtains, Nikolai guessed it was about six. He had no idea what time she needed to be up in order to get ready for the drive to the wedding. All he knew for sure was that she'd need coffee before she could do anything at all.

Edging as stealthily as possibly into her room, he checked her alarm clock. She'd set it for seven, which meant there was no use starting the coffee yet.

Violet flipped onto her back and flung an arm out onto the pillow next to her. A snuffling little snore escaped her parted lips.

He couldn't hold back a smile. For someone who exercised so much control and restraint in her waking hours, Violet slept with what could only be described as wild abandon.

Did she exercise equal abandon when she was *awake* in bed as she did when she was asleep in it?

God, what he wouldn't give to find out.

Violet sighed in her sleep and kicked a leg out of the blankets. Her sleep shorts had ridden up, revealing a delectable expanse of creamy white skin. She had a tiny strawberry-shaped birthmark on her upper, inner thigh. He wanted to trace it with his tongue.

His dick was 100% on board with *that* idea.

Nikolai cursed under his breath and tucked the blankets back around her. Falling on her like a rutting beast certainly wasn't a sound plan for making her fall in love with him.

He gave the empty spot beside her in bed one last longing glance, and turned to go.

"Soon, *kotehok*," he whispered. "Soon."

Chapter Fifteen

Even with all the fucked-up crap that was going on in her life at the moment, Violet was absurdly happy to be attending the wedding of her sister and her ex-boyfriend with an insanely hot guy who would stick by her side the entire night. If that wasn't a giant "fuck you" to the douchebag who cheated on her with her sister, then she didn't know what was.

Not that she wasn't still nervous about the whole thing. Even with Nikolai at her side, could she look her sister in the eye, smile, and offer congratulations on her wedding to a man who was willing to fuck over—literally—one sister for the other?

Yes, she thought somewhat bitterly. She would. Because that's what Violet Marchand did. She was *always* the first one to turn the other cheek. Violet had never been one to deny anyone their happiness.

Even when someone else's happiness came at the expense of her own. It was all part of the public mask she'd gotten so used to wearing.

Butterflies took flight in her stomach when Nikolai knocked on the bathroom door and asked her if she was ready to leave, which annoyed her. Damn it, this wasn't a real date, she reminded herself. Nikolai was her date because it was his job to protect her. He'd certainly made it clear that nothing else was going to happen between them anytime soon.

He knocked again when she didn't answer. "Yes," she said as she reached for the door. "I'm ready." Then she pulled the door open and her jaw practically hit the floor.

The butterflies in her stomach started fluttering about again, bumping into each other drunkenly as her gaze took him in, head to toe. He wore a charcoal-colored suit with a crisp white dress shirt and a deep red, textured silk tie. His hair was, for once, neatly combed, the scruff on his jaw gone. And had he always been so *tall*?

Holy hell, Harper had been right.

Nikolai Aleyev was *fuck hot* in a suit.

He smirked down at her. "Thank you."

Violet's chin hit her chest. "I said that out loud, didn't I?"

"Yes."

D'oh!

Well, too late to try and be cool now, she supposed. She lifted her head and let out a resigned breath.

His eyes drifted down over her dress. She was wearing the red vintage Versace she'd gotten for a song in her favorite little downtown thrift store. She was sure Lexa would approve, because Nikolai was *definitely* Versace- worthy.

"You are stunning," he said, his voice so thick with tension it made the comment sound like an understatement.

She blinked up at him. Had anyone ever called her stunning before? She didn't think so. She'd always been the smart one. The one who had to be Sabrina when she played *Charlie's Angels* with her friends, because she wasn't hot enough to play Jill. Was it anti-feminist of her to admit that in this moment, she liked being called stunning more than anything else she'd ever been called?

Swallowing hard, she turned around and gestured to her zipper. "Can you help with this?"

"Of course," he said, his voice gruff.

When his hand—huge, hot, calloused from years of hard work—touched her back, tingles shot up and down her spine. And the feel of his breath on the back of her neck as he stepped closer to move the zipper up…Jesus. Could her heart *handle* beating any faster than it was at the moment?

And was it just her, or was there something decidedly *erotic* about the rasping sound the metal teeth of the zipper made as they joined?

"There," he said after what felt like an eternity. "Got it."

She turned back around. "Thank you."

And there they stayed. In her bathroom doorway. Staring at each other.

Violet's brain screamed at her mouth to say something—anything—to break the tension. To keep from grabbing him by that silk tie, dragging his mouth down to hers and kissing him with everything she had. The way his gaze dropped to her lips made her wonder if he was having a similar internal struggle.

"So," she began, trying for a cool, breezy tone, "Are you ready for your first Marchand family event?"

His brow furrowed. "I would've said yes, but something about the way you asked that makes me wonder."

She chuckled without a trace of mirth. "All I can say for sure is that you're in for an interesting night."

He squared his shoulders and set his jaw, looking every inch the determined, stoic bodyguard. "I'm ready."

This time her laugh was 100% genuine. "You really have no idea."

Chapter Sixteen

Violet's dress, Nikolai decided, was designed for shock and awe.

And it was doing its job like a damn pro.

The crimson silk draped over her breasts and hugged the gentle curve of her hips. The skirt was shorter than what she normally wore, falling to mid-thigh. But the best—and worst—part of Violet's ensemble?

No visible panty lines.

Holy God, the view he'd get if she bent over just a tiny bit…

Fuck.

Sitting next to her—pressed to her side, thigh against thigh—in the church for what he swore was the longest wedding ceremony ever performed, had been torture. And the desire to reach over, grab her hand, and hold it in his own had been damn near overwhelming.

They'd arrived a little later than anticipated thanks to traffic on the expressway, so they'd had to sit in the back, away from Violet's mother and other sister, which was just fine with Nikolai. He was still suffering too greatly from the effects of Violet's dress to form coherent thoughts and pretend to be charming for her family.

But as he checked Violet's coat at the reception hall and helped her find their placecard, he knew he couldn't avoid socialization much longer.

Pity that.

He ushered Violet in ahead of him, taking a moment to appreciate her ass in that amazing red dress. Suddenly, she stopped and spun around, and Nikolai was pretty sure he was about to get slapped for leering at her ass, but she merely leaned into him and whispered, "That's the singles table." She gestured to a table full of sad sacks who for some reason made Nikolai think of *Island of Misfit Toys*. Wow.

"Guess I'm doing a good job of saving your life after all," he said.

Her answering smile lit up the room like the fucking sun. So beautiful.

A loud, urgent squeal cut through the din of clattering silverware, polite conversation, elevator music, and fake society laughs, almost causing Nikolai to draw his concealed Glock. Surely such a shriek was the result of someone being brutally murdered or assaulted, right?

As it turned out, no.

"Vi Vi!" the owner of the shriek of the damned called. "Thank *God* you're here!"

A pocket-sized blonde woman with a cloud of frizzy curls

and a neon orange dress so bright it hurt to look directly at it leapt up from her table—the table at which Violet and Nikolai were supposed to sit…great—and jogged on five-inch heels in their direction before launching herself into Violet's open arms.

Violet giggled and staggered backward as she seemed to catch all of the woman's weight. The sound of that giggle reached straight down into Nikolai's pants, wrapped itself right around his dick, and squeezed. Jesus. As if the dress wasn't distracting enough, now he had *that* to deal with?

"Dalia!" Violet wheezed as the other woman strengthened her hold. "It's so good to see you!"

Violet's sister, Nikolai realized. Now that he looked a little closer at the woman clinging to Violet like she was a lifeline, there was a distinct resemblance between the two of them. But the resemblance was more in their facial features than anything else. Because while Violet's dress, hair, and makeup were elegant and understated, everything about Dalia screamed…well, it just *screamed*. With her loud colors, brash voice, and heavy, vivid make-up, Dalia looked more ready for ladies' night in Vegas than she did for a tasteful wedding in upstate New York.

"Holy God, Rosie stuck us at a table with complete duds," Dalia said in a ridiculously loud stage whisper. "Making conversation with these stiffs has been *torture*!"

Several of the "stiffs" in question *harrumphed* into their drinks and turned away from the spectacle that was Dalia.

Violet shook her head and took a step back out of her sister's embrace. "You had a few drinks before we got here, didn't you, D?"

Dalia lifted her hand and blew a breath into it, sniffing delicately. Her eyes widened. "Can you smell it on me? I haven't had much. Just a smidge." She held up her thumb and index finger to indicate a smidge.

A tall man with a wry expression and eyes that sparked with intelligence behind a pair of thick, black-framed glasses stepped up and put a hand on Dalia's back. "No, honey," he said, "they can't smell it. But your lack of volume control is a fairly clear indicator of how much alcohol you've had tonight." He shot a glance at Violet and mouthed, "Three whiskey sours."

Violet sighed. "Oh, my. Looks like we're in for a loud evening." Then she leaned over and gave the man a quick hug. "Nice to see you, too, Jeff."

"Yep," Jeff said, patting her on the back before throwing an arm around Dalia. "It's been too long."

Violet turned to Nikolai. "Nikolai, you probably already figured this out, but this is my sister Dalia and her husband Jeff. Guys, this is Nikolai Aleyev."

Nikolai exchanged a handshake and a polite "nice to meet you" with Jeff, but when he held a hand out to Dalia, she merely gawked at him until Violet gave her a nudge with her shoulder. Then, Dalia blurted, "Holy Christ, what are you, an underwear model?"

So, apparently blurting out random, sometimes inappropriate thoughts was genetic. Huh. Who knew?

Jeff's chin hit his chest and Violet made a sound somewhere between a laugh and a cough.

"Um…" Nikolai started, more than a little thrown off his game by the question.

"No, Dalia," Violet said patiently, "Nikolai is not an underwear model. He's in personal security."

Violet glanced at him questioningly. He gave her a nod of approval. He saw no need to make anyone nervous by explaining his true purpose there this evening.

"Fuck," Dalia said, reaching behind her to grab her drink off the table. She downed what was left of it in one deep swallow. "I'd let you guard my *person* anytime, handsome. Know what I'm sayin'?"

Jeff sighed. "I think everyone here knows what you're saying, dear."

"I'm saying he's fucking hot," Dalia clarified unnecessarily and loudly. "Vi Vi, what's up with you showing up with a *fucking* hot guy? He's nothing like your usual type. Take Damien, for example."

"Darren," Violet corrected.

Dalia swung her arms out, chucking ice from the bottom of her glass halfway across the room, onto the dance floor, where several dancers were forced to change course before they slid through the mess. "Whatever. He's a turd. An ugly, weasel-y, greasy little turd."

"He's our brother-in-law now," Violet said.

Nikolai noticed that Violet didn't argue with Dalia's assessment that Darren was a turd. He didn't find it hard to believe, though. Anyone who would cheat on Violet couldn't be anything *but* a turd.

Dalia snorted. "That's Rose's problem, not ours. Looks like you traded up big time, little sis."

Nikolai couldn't hold back a small smirk, but he inclined his head in a formal, proper way and said, "You're too kind. I thank you."

Her eyes widened. "Fuck, that accent's hot, too." She turned to Violet. "I'll bet you can come just *listening* to that."

Jeff nudged his glasses up with his index finger and pinched the bridge of his nose. "You know I'm standing right here, don't you?"

Dalia leaned over to pinch his cheek, but missed and ended up poking him in the nose with her thumb. "Love you, baby," she slurred, then made sloppy-sounding kissing noises in his direction.

Somehow, Violet managed to guide her inebriated sister to their table and pour her into a chair. Jeff went back to the bar to fetch his wife a much-needed cup of coffee. Violet smiled her thanks up at Nikolai when he pulled her chair out for her.

And there it was again. That simultaneous punch to the gut and balls that Violet managed with nothing more than a word or smile in his direction. How the hell did she *do* that?

"Thank you for coming with me to this thing," she said as he took a seat next to her. "I know you must be miserable."

Don't do it, he told himself. *Don't be an idiot.*

Nikolai leaned closer and was gratified by her quick intake of breath. At least he wasn't alone in this...*attraction* they had. He eased a curl that had escaped her complicated up-do behind her ear, letting his fingertips trail across her cheekbone.

"I'm exactly where I want to be," he whispered in her ear.

She pulled back, and the look she shot him was so full of *want* it made him lightheaded. (Having all of your blood head south of your belt could do that to a man.)

Thank God for long tablecloths, he thought wryly. At least no one else would realize what a masochistic dumbass he was for failing ass-over-elbow for a woman who may never be ready to love him back, or even let him see the *real* her he knew she kept so closely guarded.

So apparently it was too late for him to avoid being an idiot.

Pity that.

Chapter Seventeen

Over the next hour, Nikolai was a study in patience and tolerance.

He listened politely to Jeff's rambling stories about his co-workers at the elementary school where he taught math. He didn't get irritated when Dalia took every possible opportunity to grope him ("Oh, you've got a piece of schmutz on your jacket. Here, let me rub that off for you. Ha! Rub that off. See what I did there? It's a play on 'rub one off?'") He made sure everyone at the table—even the stiffs—had fresh drinks whenever they wanted them. And he did it all while looking *fuck hot* and surreptitiously surveying the room for possible threats to her safety.

In short, Nikolai was the perfect wedding date. It was like he was going for some kind of wedding date sainthood, as a matter of fact.

Violet leaned toward him and asked, "Any signs of trouble?"

He rested an arm on the back of her chair and shook his head. "None," he said quietly. "Except your mother keeps giving me really strange looks I can't interpret."

Violet raised a brow. "I'm in my early thirties, unmarried, and I show up at a wedding with a guy who looks like *you*. There's nothing to interpret. To her, you're walking sperm, heaven-sent to give her grandchildren." She shrugged. "Sorry."

He should just be happy her mother had been too busy helping the event coordinators make sure everything was perfect for Rose's reception to spend too much time at their table. Violet could only imagine the kinds of embarrassing questions her mother would grill them with.

His answering smirk would've weakened her knees if she'd been standing. "What about you, *kotehok*? Tell me the truth. The whole stalking and attempted murder was a ploy to get me where you really want me, wasn't it?"

The giggle that escaped her was so girlish and embarrassing she clapped a hand over her mouth to keep it from getting any worse.

Nikolai's pupils dilated as he leaned in closer to her and pulled her hand away from her mouth. He pressed a kiss to her knuckles and the brush of his breath across her skin nearly set her panties on fire.

Holy. Hell.

"I've been waiting a lifetime for you to give me that laugh," he said gruffly. "Don't deny me."

I'm done denying you anything.

The words wanted to roll off her tongue, but Violet held them back out of sheer force of habit. What was wrong with her? Why couldn't she just let go for once and give up the calm, cool façade? Here was this beautiful man, looking at her with his heart in his eyes, being nothing but open and honest with her, even though she knew it was hard for him, and she just couldn't let herself tell him how she felt about…well, anything, really. It was ridiculous.

She swallowed hard. "Nikolai, I—"

Whatever Violet was going to say was cut off by a shriek she knew all too well. And this time it wasn't Dalia's happy-go-lucky, drunken shriek. Nope. It was way worse than that.

"Violet!"

Taking a deep, fortifying breath, Violet stood and turned to face her other sister, but pulled up short when Rose shoved what looked to be a three-carat, princess-cut diamond solitaire and wedding band under her nose.

"Isn't it just gorgeous?" Rose said, waving her fingers under Violet's nose. "Doesn't Darren just have the *most* exquisite taste?"

"Not from where I'm sitting," Nikolai muttered under his breath.

Violet nearly bit her tongue in half trying to hold back the laughter that threatened to bubble up out of her throat. Fortunately (and not surprisingly), Rose was oblivious as she continued to flaunt her ring.

"Yes, Rose," Violet agreed dutifully. "It's a lovely ring. The ceremony was perfect as well. Congratulations."

Rose stopped waving her ring around and laid a hand on Violet's shoulder. "I know this must be so, so hard for you," she said, her voice brimming with an *attempt* at sympathy.

Violet knew it was only an *attempt*, though, because her sister's eyes were brimming with glee. At the thought of laying permanent claim to something that was once Violet's, or because it was her wedding day, Violet had no idea. Knowing her history with Rose, it was most likely the former.

Violet did her level best to radiate zero hard feelings or jealousy in Rose's direction. "It's not hard for me at all, Rose. It's wonderful to see you so happy."

Rose's enthusiasm dimmed a bit at that. "Oh…well…that's great. Thank you. It would absolutely break my heart if you hated me because of what happened."

"You mean how you fucked her boyfriend in her house while she was upstairs sleeping? 'Cause that's what happened, right?" Dalia asked, her whiskey-laced voice reaching a volume that could most likely be heard by every guest in the room and half the kitchen staff.

Rose's upper lip curled up into a Billy Idol-esque snarl. "Classy, Dalia. Just like always."

Dalia snorted and tossed back what had to be her fifth whiskey sour, ignoring the coffee her husband kept surreptitiously nudging in front of her. "I'm just keeping it real, princess. And don't act like you aren't just trying to get a rise out of Vi Vi. Go back to your dipshit husband and leave us alone," she said, making a shooing motion with her hand and managing to slap Jeff in the face.

Jeff adjusted the glasses Dalia had knocked askew on his nose and snatched the glass out of her hand. He shoved his own glass of water over to her. "I'm officially cutting you off."

She blew a raspberry at him like an agitated chimp and turned back to Rose. "Besides, it won't work, Rosey Posey. 'Cause why the fuck would Vi Vi be jealous of *Darren* when she's sitting here with a fucking underwear model?"

Pretty much every eye in the room swiveled in Nikolai's direction at that point.

Jeff winced. "Sorry, man."

Nikolai, calm and cool as ever, merely stood up and offered Rose his hand. "Nikolai Aleyev," he said. "It's a pleasure to meet you."

His tone said exactly the opposite, though, Violet noted. It would seem that Nikolai was unimpressed by her little sister. Very interesting, she thought.

Violet hadn't met a single man in her entire life who hadn't been impressed by Rose. With her delicate, fine-boned features, Angelina Jolie lips, wild cloud of auburn curls, and lithe, athletic little body, Rose was nothing short of stunning. And at the moment, she kind of looked like wedding Barbie. What guy could resist a walking fantasy like Rose?

Nikolai Aleyev, apparently.

Violet had an almost insatiable urge to grab him by the back of the neck and kiss the stuffing out of him for that alone.

Rose immediately switched off her "bitchy sister" mode and downshifted directly into "maneater" as she stared up at Nikolai. Violet knew all the signs of flirty Rose. The slight head tilt. The way she touched the tip of her tongue to her upper lip like a hungry kitten. The wide green eyes and look that spoke of hot summer nights, sweaty skin, and promises of lots and lots of nudity. Yep. Violet had pretty much seen Rose direct this same look towards every guy she'd ever brought home with her when she was in college and grad school.

Reaction from the guys was pretty standard, too. There was a handshake that went on a little too long, followed by sweat beading on their brow, finished off with a subtle crotch adjustment. Violet glanced up at Nikolai, steeling herself. She couldn't even *pretend* it wasn't going to hurt if Nikolai flirted with Rose.

"It's such a *pleasure* to meet *you*," Rose purred. "And you're Violet's…"

Violet panicked for a moment. What was he supposed to say? Bodyguard? Guy who kidnapped her that one time? Dream boy toy?

Nikolai glanced down at Violet before saying, "Yes. I'm Violet's. 100%."

"Holy shit," Dalia blurted out behind them. "That's so fucking hot," she stage-whispered, then gave Nikolai a thumbs up, along with an encouraging smile.

He smiled back at her and gave her a wink. Dalia choked on the sip of water she'd just taken and turned to her husband. "I think I just came."

Jeff rested an elbow on the table and let his forehead drop into his waiting palm. "Jesus," he muttered.

Rose continued making small talk with Nikolai while Jeff tried to talk Dalia into eating some bread to soak up all the alcohol in her system, but Violet barely heard any of them over the ringing in her ears.

The way Nikolai said he was hers had been *perfect*. And he hadn't said it just for Rose's benefit. She didn't know *how* she knew that, but she did.

He'd meant every word. How had she missed this? He'd said just last night that they couldn't be together until the threat against her had been neutralized…but something in the way he was looking at her now told her he could be convinced otherwise.

She was *sure* all she had to do was talk to him, let her walls down, and let him know she wanted him. All that heat and passion—

and possibly *love*—would be *hers*.

And she wanted it. God, how she wanted it.

What the hell was she waiting for?

"Nikolai," she began again, putting her hand on his arm.

He immediately turned away from Rose and leaned down towards her a bit. "What's the matter, *kotehok*?"

I want you. I want you now. I've always wanted you. I don't want to wait another minute to have you.

She opened her mouth, but the words stuck in her throat again. Damn it! Why the hell couldn't she just say it?

He frowned, looking concerned. "Are you feeling alright? You look a bit pale."

"It's just the red dress," Rose said dismissively. "Bright colors have always washed her out.

Violet bit back an uncharitable reply.

It's your sister's wedding day. Let her have her perfect moment.

Ugh. Now she was hearing her mother's voice in her head. That couldn't be normal, could it?

Nikolai was still looking down at her, frowning, so she shook her head. "I'm fine. I just—"

"Well, well," a dry, pompous voice interrupted. "Look who we have here."

Rose squealed with delight and clapped her hands together like a little girl on Christmas morning. Nikolai turned and raised an eyebrow at the newcomer, clearly not as impressed as Rose. Meanwhile, Violet felt the filet she'd had for dinner start to sour in her stomach. Wishing she could make a run for the door but knowing she'd never make it in her damn heels and tight dress, Violet turned, resigned to her fate, and looked right at the face of the one person—other than the guy who wanted to kill her, of course—she'd hoped to avoid all night.

"Hello, Darren," she said.

"Vi." Darren's gaze immediately dropped to her cleavage and he licked his lips. Violet's skin crawled as if someone had just dumped a bucket of spiders down the back of her dress. "You look delicious tonight."

The emphasis he put on the word delicious was creepy and lecherous and not at all brother-in-law-like. Gross.

On second thought, she'd rather face the guy who wanted to kill her than this tool.

Chapter Eighteen

Harper had told Nikolai the entire story of Violet's history with Darren to prep him for this wedding. He'd listened carefully, but surely, either he or Harper had gotten something wrong.

Because on what planet could a douchebag like *this* get Violet to go out with him for a single date, let alone date her steadily for months? It didn't make any damn sense.

Darren didn't bother to even look in his direction, so Nikolai took the opportunity to size the bastard up.

He wasn't that tall. Maybe 5'9" or so. Average build. Lean, but not muscular. Plain features. Nothing extraordinary at all. And his hair looked absolutely ridiculous. Nikolai wasn't exactly up on trends in male fashion, but he didn't imagine Caesar cuts were in style anywhere in the world at the moment.

And yet this doofus had seen Violet naked and Nikolai hadn't. Was there no justice in the world?

"Bawhoosh!" Dalia called out. "Bawhoosh!"

Jeff groaned. "What now?"

Dalia pointed to Darren. "I'm trying to flush the turd! Bawhoosh!" She made a little flushing motion with her index and middle finger.

It took Nikolai a second or two to figure out that *bawhoosh* was Dalia's drunken impression of a toilet. He couldn't hold back a little chuckle.

"Don't encourage her, man," Jeff said, shoving another mug of coffee under his wife's nose.

"Just ignore her," Rose said with a sneer. "That's what I try to do."

Darren didn't seem to have any trouble ignoring Dalia and Jeff. His full attention was centered on Violet. And her sexy little red dress, of course. What kind of asshole leers at his sister-in-law on his wedding day?

Violet didn't waste time on pleasantries with Darren, Nikolai noticed. Instead of greeting or congratulating him, Violet just looped her arm through Nikolai's and said, "Darren, this is Nikolai. Nikolai, this is Rose's husband, Darren."

Not *"this is the loser who had me and was dumb enough to screw it all up and hurt me in the process,"* but *"Rose's husband."* And she said it a tone that implied *he's her problem now, not mine, thank God.* Nikolai liked that. It was good hearing absolutely no pain or longing in her voice as she addressed the—how did Harper say it?—*twatwaffle*.

If he thought Violet held even an inkling of warm feelings for Darren, Nikolai would most likely have to break the guy's legs. Or maybe his arms and legs. Snapping his neck and spine would probably be overkill (so to speak), right?

Nikolai's musings were interrupted when Darren shoved a hand in his direction. "Nice to meet you, man," the idiot said with absolutely zero sincerity.

And not only was he *not* pleased to meet Nikolai, but his beady little eyes immediately shifted back to Violet's cleavage after meeting Nikolai's for a cursory moment.

Maybe snapping his neck and/or back wouldn't be overkill after all.

Nikolai took Darren's hand, silently praying the other man would be dumb enough to get aggressive with him. It didn't take but a second for Darren to tighten his hand in what he probably thought was a crushing grip.

He had no idea.

With a smirk, Nikolai tightened his own grip, putting only about 20 percent of his strength behind it. That 20 percent was enough that he felt the bones in Darren's hand shift and grind together under the pressure. Darren's skin paled and sweat beaded on his forehead. Nikolai bared his teeth in what he hoped Violet wouldn't notice was a warning instead of a smile.

"Nice to meet you, too," he said, giving Darren's hand one last painful squeeze before releasing him.

Rose rushed to explain to Darren that Nikolai was Violet's boyfriend and kept babbling about…something. Nikolai quit listening. The girl was apparently so wrapped up in the sound of her own voice that she failed to notice her new husband rubbing his hand, probably trying to get some feeling back in it. Good luck with that, dumbass, Nikolai thought. That hand would be numb for the rest of the night and would most likely be too sore to use tomorrow.

The thought made Nikolai smile again.

As Rose prattled on to no one in particular, beside him, Violet sighed. "I can't believe you did that *again*," she whispered.

"Did what?" he asked as innocently as he could manage.

She shot him a reproachful look that he returned with a shrug. Eventually, her stern face relaxed and she said, "You didn't have to do that, but…thank you."

Her tiny hint of a smile meant more to him than glowing praise from anyone else on earth. "You know I'd do anything for you," he answered.

Surely the unnatural shine in her eyes at his words was a trick of the candlelight, right?

"You know, I think I'm beginning to understand that," she said quietly.

An hour later, feeling confident that they'd done their time and that her mother couldn't claim she'd bailed too early, Violet was more than ready to go home. Nikolai went to get her coat while she went to the bathroom one last time before they hit the road.

Of course, he'd refused to let her go in alone until he'd checked the stalls to make sure no one was hiding in there and planning to strangle her, à la *Copycat*. Violet was a little ashamed to admit she was grateful to Nikolai for that. She'd had an irrational fear of public bathrooms—and Harry Connick, Jr., if she was being honest—since 1995 because of that movie.

But when she was done and headed back out to say goodnight to Dalia, it wasn't Nikolai she found waiting for her in the hallway right outside the ladies' room. Violet tried valiantly to keep all the *ugh* off her face as she gave him a polite nod of acknowledgement and attempted to brush past him.

Darren, clueless as ever to social cues and graces, it would seem, grabbed her wrist. "Violet, I'm so glad you came. I've been wanting to apologize for how things went down between us for a long time."

Violet swallowed her first-instinct reply of "Oh, you didn't ever go down on me, remember? That was my *sister's* thighs I found your head between when I got up for a glass of water that night," opting instead for a simple, "It's all ancient history, Darren. There's no reason to apologize now."

"It's not like an apology from a sister-fucker like you means shit anyhow," Dalia said, elbowing them out of her way as she stumbled into the bathroom. And with that, she lifted her middle finger in Darren's direction, then kicked the bathroom door shut behind her.

Well, guess there's not much more to say than that, is there?

Violet gave Darren's shoulder a pat, congratulated him on his marriage one last time, and turned to go. But once again, he didn't take the hint and his grip on her wrist tightened.

"No, I mean it, Vi," he said, giving her a sad-eyed look that reminded her of Antonio Banderas's character in *Puss in Boots*. "I was so wrong to betray you like that."

Yes, you were. "Really, Darren, I'm over it. No worries."

He let out a deep breath and smiled. "I'm so glad. I just hate thinking you might still be hurt about us, you know? It makes me feel awful."

And I'd just hate for you *to feel awful about potentially hurting me, now, years and years after you fucked my sister.*

Self-absorbed prick. Had he always been this much of an asshole and she'd just overlooked it?

Violet smiled politely and again attempted to pull her wrist out of his grip. Again, he didn't let her go.

He glanced at her cleavage again, then down at the floor. "Well, I just…this is awkward for me. But I guess I'll just say it. Vi, honey, what the hell are you doing with that guy?"

Violet let her polite smile dip. "What do you mean?"

"Vi," he said again, leaning forward, "You being with someone like *him*…does this have anything to do with me marrying Rosie?"

Violet felt a frown line grooving its way across her brow. Had she had too much to drink? Was *that* why his words weren't making any sense? "I don't understand, Darren."

He shook his head. "This guy isn't right for you, Vi. A security guard? Come on, you can do way better than that and you know it. He's so far beneath you. I have to wonder if you're just…if you were just desperate or something because of the wedding."

This must be what an aneurysm feels like, Violet thought. One minute you're completely fine, and the next, something in your head is quite literally exploding. "*You* think I can do better? *You* think I'm desperate? You think *he's* beneath me?"

He winced at the bite in her tone. "I just still care so much about you, Violet. I only want what's best for you."

The smile that stretched across her face at his words felt so brittle she was sure it was going to crack at any moment. "Well, Darren, it's *terribly* kind of you to be so concerned about me, but there's no need. You know why? As it turns out, my love life is no longer any of your business."

Darren gave her a sad smile and a little nod. "It's my loss."

Ugh. Gag. This time, she tugged hard enough on her wrist that he had no choice but to let her go. He held his hands up in surrender under the weight of the glare she hit him with.

"It's just that...how well do you know this guy, Vi?" Darren added, giving his head another sad shake. "I don't trust him. There's something shifty about him."

She spluttered. "There's something shifty about *him*? *Him*? *You* think there's something shifty about *him*?"

He opened his mouth to say something else, but she cut him off. "You want to know what I know about him? Fair enough. For starters, I know he's not fucking my sister. That's a huge plus in my book."

His cheeks flushed, but he acknowledged, "True, but—"

"You know what else I know about him?" she said, injecting as much *shut the fuck up* into her tone as possible. "I know that he's honest and smart and funny and so damn sexy it hurts to look at him sometimes."

"Well, I—"

"I'm not done. I also know he's the type of man who'd take a bullet for me. Who'd die before letting anything hurt me. So when you say I can do better?" She let out a short, angry bark of sarcastic laughter. "I say there is *no one* better than Nikolai Aleyev. *You*, asshole, are not even fit to breathe *his* air."

Dalia shoved the bathroom door open and let out a huge burp before saying, "Amen, sister."

She gave Violet a palm-stinging high-five before tottering back to her table.

The interruption helped Violet rein in her anger somewhat. At least, she was starting to get it under control until he said, "God, Vi, I don't think I've ever seen you get angry like that before. It's so fucking *hot*."

That's when Violet actually started to feel her blood boil. It pounded through her veins with an unnatural intensity, making a roaring noise in her ears. Her entire life—a life spent doing the right thing, being the mature, responsible adult in the room, being in charge, being the cool, collected one in a crisis—flashed before her eyes. When did *she* get to be the emotional one? When did Violet finally get what *she* wanted? Her right eye twitched and her hands clenched into fists.

Right in this moment, that's when. Today. Fucking *today*.

"Well, if you liked that, you're going to love this," she growled.

With that, she drew back her arm and threw her first-ever punch at someone.

And she was feeling pretty good about it, if she did say so herself…until Nikolai caught her fist a split second before it connected with Darren's nose.

"I can't let you do that," Nikolai said calmly.

"Oh, come on," she whined. "He deserves it! Did you hear what he said to me? About you?"

He nodded. "Yes, he deserves it, and yes, I heard every word. But I can't let you punch him like that."

Her shoulders slumped. "I know violence isn't the answer, and punching someone in the face isn't a mature response, but—"

Nikolai lifted her still-clenched hand and said, "If you hit him like this, with your thumb tucked inside your fist, you'll really hurt yourself. Your thumb will snap like a twig." He pried her hand open, then curled her fingers closed again with her thumb on the outside. "There. That's how your fist should look when you throw a punch."

She blinked up at him. "You mean…you don't want to stop me?"

He snorted. "I did stop you. I stopped you from breaking your thumb. Now, when you throw your punch, turn into it from your hip. Like this." He pulled her fist forward with one hand, and twisted her hip in the same direction with his other hand. "That way, you're putting all your weight into the punch. And don't just stop when you make contact. Imagine you're trying to punch *through* his nose. Really follow through, yes?"

Darren rolled his eyes. "Oh, come on. We both know she's not *really* going to—"

Violet threw her punch. She did exactly what Nikolai said, and when her fist connected with Darren's nose and she felt bone and cartilage snap under the pressure, it was indescribable. The power, the release of anger, the feeling of hurting someone who'd hurt her…it was the best damn thing she'd felt in a long, long time.

"Ow! You broke my nose!"

"I did," Violet whispered, marveling at the blood now trickling down the front of his dress shirt. She whirled to face Nikolai. "I did it!"

She'd been wrong, she knew immediately. Punching Darren wasn't the best feeling she'd had in a long time, because the proud smile Nikolai was giving her blew that feeling out of the water.

"That was beautiful, *kotehok*," he murmured, his accent thicker than usual. "Absolutely perfect. Just like you."

And that's when all the fear and confusion and anxiousness she'd been carrying around with her evaporated completely.

It was time. She'd been a damn fool to wait as long as she had.

"I want you," Violet blurted out before she could lose her

nerve again. "I don't care about the past. I don't care about the future or the death threats or anything else. I just want you. Tonight. Now."

Not exactly an elegant speech, but apparently it was good enough for Nikolai. His green eyes immediately darkened, crackling with heat.

"It's about damn time," he growled, grabbing her hand and dragging her to the door like the place was on fire.

"Oh, no, you don't," Rose hissed, grabbing Violet's wrist. "You think you can act like that, ruin *my* day, hit *my* husband, and just walk away?"

Nikolai let go of Violet's hand and moved to position himself between them, but Violet stopped him. She was still riding high on the thrill of letting her mask slip for a time. It'd felt *so* good that there was *no way* she was going to miss the opportunity to say a few things to her sister. "I've got this."

"Quickly," he urged, his expression hovering somewhere between irritated at the interruption and desperate to leave.

Violet *totally* understood the urgency.

She turned back to her sister. "Rose, you're my sister and I love you."

"You can't just—"

Violet laid her index finger over her sister's lips. "I'm not done, sweetheart. You're my sister and I love you. But I don't *like* you at all. You were a rotten little girl, and you've grown into a petty, spiteful, *hateful* woman. And when your looks go, you'll be nothing but a bitter old hag, and I don't want to see that happen to you."

Rose sucked in an outraged gasp and flushed a shade of red Violet thought might have even been deeper than the hue of her Versace. In her head, Violet heard Mr. Burns from the *Simpsons* saying, "Excellent," while tenting his fingers devilishly. That voice—and her desire to get out of this pit of despair and have some *real* fun with Nikolai—urged her on. "You're also a selfish, jealous, conceited, bratty…" she trailed off, searching for the right word.

"Twatwaffle?" Nikolai suggested helpfully.

Violet grinned at him before turning back to her sister. "Twatwaffle," she finished with a flourish. "And your husband was hitting on me and staring at my cleavage. So, good luck with all that. Hope you get it all straightened out. See you at Christmas."

And with that, Violet grabbed Nikolai's hand and pulled him out the door.

"I thought you punching Darren was the hottest thing I'd ever seen," Nikolai said as he held the car door open for her. "But that was…" he trailed off, shaking his head.

"Fuck hot?" she suggested.

"Yes," he agreed immediately.

"Good. I'll pay dearly for that when my mom hears about it, but it was *totally* worth it."

Chapter Nineteen

Traffic laws—and possible a few land speed records—were broken as they tore out of the reception hall's parking lot and began the long drive back to Violet's apartment.

Nikolai grabbed one of her hands, dropped a kiss on her knuckles, then laced his fingers through hers. He rested their linked hands on his thigh and kept his other hand on the wheel. "Talk to me," he said. "Tell me everything I've always wanted to know about you."

Violet didn't need any further clarification. She already knew what he wanted to hear. "My public mask," she whispered.

He side-eyed her, almost as if he didn't believe she was really going to tell him anything, but kept his mouth shut, giving her only a quick nod.

She shifted in her seat so she could watch his gorgeous profile while she spoke. God, how had she resisted him this long? She'd been *such* an idiot.

"My father died when I was ten," she began, shocked to find that such an old memory still had the power to cause her pain. "Heart attack."

Nikolai's fingers tightened on hers, offering silent support.

"He'd been the breadwinner for our family," she went on.

"My mom stayed home to take care of me and my sisters. We didn't have much money before he died, no insurance or anything, and after he was gone…well, things got worse."

Violet gave Nikolai the Cliff's Notes version of her childhood in the months after her father's death. They'd lost their home, lived in the family Buick for a few weeks, and eventually found their way into a homeless shelter where a few good Samaritans helped her mother put together a resume and nail down some job interviews. Her mom was smart and hardworking, and it didn't take long for her to get an administrative job with a small law firm in Hell's Kitchen.

They were out of the homeless shelter and in a new apartment close to her mother's office a few weeks later. They were so lucky. Violet could still remember the tiny bedroom she'd shared with her sisters, and how when she'd first seen it, she'd asked her mother if they were rich now, because that tiny little apartment that smelled of old takeout Chinese food, was practically a Beverly Hills mansion compared to where they'd come from.

Her mother had laughed a deep, hearty laugh, and with tears in her eyes, she'd replied, "Yes, baby. We have a roof over our heads and food in our bellies, and we have each other. There's no one richer than us."

But despite their drastic improvement in circumstances, their lives were still far from perfect. Her mother's administrative job was great, but it didn't pay nearly enough to cover their living expenses, so she'd picked up a second job at night, waiting tables at a bar downtown.

From that point on, Violet was in charge of the regular household duties—not by choice, but by necessity. Dalia was older, but she was wild. Always breaking curfew, drinking, smoking, boys…name a stereotypical reckless teenager behavior and Dalia was all over it. And Rose was just a baby, which left Violet to take on the role of responsible, serious adult.

"When Rose needed shots and checkups," she told Nikolai, "it was my responsibility to get her there. When Dalia was flunking math, it was my job to help her study and get her grades back up. When we didn't have rent money, it was up to me to talk to the building super and get an extension."

He kept his eyes on the road but frowned severely enough to make her laugh. "It wasn't nearly as bad as it sounds. There were certainly plenty of kids in the neighborhood who had it worse. But my childhood taught me just how important my mask was for getting what I wanted."

His frown remained intact. "What do you mean?"

"I mean, Dalia was fun and exciting and vibrant, so she got what she wanted by charming people with her personality. Rose was young and adorable, so she got what she wanted using her looks. I got what I wanted by being smart, calm, rational, and professional. By not letting anyone know how I was *really* feeling about anything. By being in control."

He let go of her hand to brush his thumb across her cheekbone and she shivered at the gentleness of the gesture. "And the fancy clothes and pulled-back hair complete the mask, huh?"

She offered him a sad smile. "Pretty much. I've always had the need to be taken seriously. I needed adults to see me as another adult, even when I was a kid, because I was in charge of my family when my mom was working, which was all the time. And the mask just kind of stuck with me through adulthood." Violet shrugged. "I guess I got used to it. It became comfortable for me."

"And if you could just be yourself? If you didn't need the mask anymore? Would you still wear it?"

In lieu of an answer, she pulled the pins out of her hair and ran her fingers through it to fluff it up. She couldn't help but sigh with pleasure as her hair tumbled down around her shoulders. God, it felt good to get those pins out. Almost orgasmic. Kind of like taking off a push-up bra after a long day.

When she glanced back over at him, he held her gaze longer than was probably a good idea, considering he was driving. But the heat and intensity in his expression was so overwhelming she couldn't bring herself to care.

A muscle in his jaw twitched as he shifted his gaze back to the road, and he hit the gas, causing the car to lurch forward. She couldn't help but smile. She completely understood his urgency. If they didn't get back to her place, if she couldn't get skin to skin with him soon, she was pretty sure she might actually die from wanting him.

"I'm the first you've let see beneath the mask," he said, his low, rumbly voice causing a thousand butterflies to take flight in her belly.

"Yes," she whispered. She was showing him pieces of herself, of her history, that she'd never shown to even her best friends and family. It was scary and exhilarating all at the same time.

He nodded, looking lost in thought, before saying, "Tell me more."

"What else did you want to know?"

"The dogs," he answered.

Ah, yes, the reason she stopped at the pound every week, spent hours playing with every dog there, but never took one home. "You'll think it's silly," she warned.

She shifted her gaze out the window even though it was dark outside and she couldn't really see anything, save the occasional blur of lights as they passed through various little towns and pockets of civilization.

"I always wanted a dog when I was growing up," she

admitted. "We could never afford to have one, so I always said that as soon as I was out of school, the first thing I was going to do was adopt a dog. I went to do exactly that—on my graduation day, I stopped at the pound on my way home. And I just couldn't do it. There's so many dogs there, and they all have these horrible backstories. They all need good homes, so I can't ever decide which one to take with me when I leave. I guess I just feel guilty about leaving the others behind. Like I'm letting them down by not choosing them, you know?"

When he remained quiet, she grumbled, "See? Silly."

"*Nyet*," he said, his voice thick with emotion. "You have a tender heart. There's nothing silly about that. I think it's beautiful. You're beautiful."

He reached over again and grabbed her hand, pressing another kiss to the center of her palm. The feel of his warm lips on her skin was nothing short of panty-melting.

And having his mouth in the same sentence with her panties had her heart fluttering.

"And the homeless man you visit?" he asked.

"Lester is a war vet," Violet told him. "Iraq. He has stories that are absolutely heartbreaking. I've been covertly giving him PTSD therapy for two years now. I don't think he realizes what I'm doing, and I kind of feel bad about it because he never asked for my help, but…"

"It's what you do," he whispered. "If someone is hurting, you help them."

She shrugged. "It's in my DNA, I guess. Didn't you have one more thing you always wanted to know? Something about why I wasn't with anyone?"

He smiled. "Ah, that's the really tricky question, isn't it?"

Violet swallowed hard. "Not really. I'm starting to think…maybe I was just waiting for the right person. Maybe I was waiting for you."

He sucked in a deep breath. "Thank God. Because I'm not going anywhere. Not unless you tell me to go."

Chapter Twenty

They didn't talk much after Violet spilled her guts. Mostly, Nikolai completely clammed up when she put her hand on his thigh. She couldn't help it. She just had to touch him. After that, his jaw clenched and no more words were exchanged. Violet was fine with that. It gave her time to think.

And what she decided after all that *thinking* was that she was *done* thinking.

When they finally got home, Nikolai threw the car in park and shifted in his seat to face her. "I know we still have a lot to talk about, and—"

"No."

He frowned at her. "No?"

"No, we're not talking. Not right now, anyway."

He ran a hand over his jaw, which already sported some impressive five o'clock shadow. Violet could only imagine how wonderful that would feel against her skin. "I'm not looking for more heavy conversation right now. We can do that later. Right now I just want to be with you. I'm tired of thinking. I just want to *feel*. Don't you want that, too?"

His gaze heated and tingles shot through her entire body, right down to her toes. "There's nothing I want more in this world."

Was it her imagination, or was he starting to lean ever so slightly closer to her? If so, thank you, Jesus. "Really?"

"Really. I've never wanted to kiss anyone as badly as I want to kiss you right now."

Those fiery tingles shot up her thighs. He closed the distance between them then, his eyes locked on her lips. "But we should definitely talk more first."

Frustration nearly choked her. "Look, I know it's a good idea to talk first. It's the right thing to do. But I'm tired of doing the right thing—the sensible, *logical* thing. I want to do what *feels* good, and what feels good—what feels *right* now—is being with you. Please kiss me."

She didn't have to tell him twice. His strong hands angled her head and his mouth captured hers, the stroke of his tongue against hers nearly causing her to melt into a puddle of lust right there in her own car.

Violet pulled back just enough to whisper, "Come inside with me. Now."

He groaned when she slid her fingers up to the top of his thighs. When he didn't make any attempt to stop her, she brushed her thumb over the impressive ridge of his erection, shocking even herself with her newfound boldness.

"Fucking hell," he whispered.

Her heart pounded as they practically sprinted from the car into her building. Violet fumbled with her keys, hands shaking, while Nikolai slid his warm hands under her skirt, fingers skimming up her thighs. She let out a choked gasp as his mouth descended on her neck, his lips hot on her skin.

By some miracle, she managed to get the door open and Nikolai kicked it shut behind them. They moved as one through her tiny foyer and into the living room, Nikolai at her back, making quick work of the buttons on her coat, all while his tongue did things to her neck that wobbled her knees.

When her coat was unbuttoned, he tossed it onto the couch before spinning her around and crowding her against the wall. There—right there against her living room wall—they made out like teenagers, feeding each other hot, open-mouthed kisses, groping and grappling until they were both panting and breathless with need.

Time seemed to stand still. It could've been minutes or hours that they writhed against each other—Violet didn't know, and she wasn't sure she cared.

He pulled back just enough to rest his forehead against hers, his breathing as labored as her own. "Are you sure?" He sounded like he'd swallowed broken glass. "No turning back. I've wanted you from the moment I saw you. Dreamed of you, imagined you every night." He bit his bottom lip and she had an inexplicable urge to replace his teeth with her own on that lush, plump flesh. "So, yes or no, Violet. Either way is fine with me, but you have to be sure."

He was giving her every opportunity to back away, to put on the brakes, all while looking like a rejection from her could kill him. But still, he was handing all the power, all the control, over to her. It was a beautiful gesture that proved just how well he knew her.

A beautiful gesture, but an unnecessary one. There was really only one answer she could give him. She'd been ready for this moment since the first time she saw him outside that coffee shop all those months ago.

"Yes," she whispered. "I'm sure I want you. I *need* you."

Then his mouth was on hers in what could only be called a claiming, and she was more than willing to offer him everything she had, everything she was.

Just to make sure her intentions were perfectly clear—and since she'd gotten such a perfect reaction from him in the car—Violet reached between them and rubbed her palm over his erection. He spit out a tangle of urgent-sounding Russian, then slid his hands down to cup her ass and pull her against him. She shifted and opened her mouth against his throat, flicking her tongue against his skin.

And, God, he tasted amazing.

Violet was so turned on she could barely breathe. Or maybe the electricity and heat between them was sucking all the air out of the room? She wasn't sure. But if the foreplay was nearly killing her, how was she supposed to survive when she finally got this man inside her?

He must have seen the questions in her eyes because he flashed her a wolfish grin that all but screamed *you* can *take it and you* will *take it all*. Then he spun her around, pressing her front into the wall.

Before she'd processed the change in positions, her dress hit the floor, pooling at her feet. Violet let out a nervous gasp and flattened her palms against the wall for support. The new, bold, and wild Violet fled the building for a moment, and the old Violet took over, feeling a little embarrassed.

Underwear hadn't been possible with her dress if she wanted to avoid panty lines. It made sense while she was getting dressed, but now that she was completely naked against the wall in front of the most physically perfect man she'd ever seen, with the *lights* on, for God's sake.

All her self-consciousness scattered when Nikolai pressed up against her back, sliding his hands down her thighs, then nudging them apart.

"You're so beautiful, Violet," he whispered in her ear before gently nipping her earlobe. "I've never seen anything so perfect."

He slid his hand down and pressed the heel of his hand against her swollen clit. "You feel perfect, too," he murmured. "So hot and wet."

She bucked back against him as he slowly—so, so slowly—slid a finger through her wet folds and into her, pinning her against him. Violet pressed against the wall again to keep her balance when her knees threatened to buckle. "Oh, my God. Please, Nikolai. Now," she cried out.

"No. I've waited far too long for you to rush now."

He was trying to kill her, she decided. There was no possible way she could take much more of this. Then he slid a second finger into her and she bit down on her lower lip to keep from letting out what would surely be a wail, quickly followed by more begging for him to put her out of her sensual misery.

But by now, the new Violet was back in control and she wasn't about to just sit back and let Nikolai do all the work. She intended to make him every bit as crazy as he was making her.

Violet laid her hand over his, arching back into him again. He moaned as she bucked against his questing fingers and turned her face into his neck.

As his fingers moved, she reached back and threaded her hands through his hair so that she had an anchor to reality. Every stroke of his tongue against hers, every slide of his fingers, every time his hand tightened on her hip, pushed her higher and higher until she was so wet and ready he could probably make her come just by ordering her to.

Then he pulled his fingers away and she cried out at the loss.

"I'm not going anywhere, *kotehok*," he whispered. "Put your hands back on the wall and arch your back."

Violet hurried to do as she was told, but glanced back at him over her shoulder just in time to see him grab her ass and bury his face between her thighs to…

Oh. God.

She definitely wasn't going to survive this.

She choked out his name on a broken wail as his tongue slid down over her folds and flicked against her clit. Violet went up on her toes and spread her legs further apart, arched back a little more to give him better access. This might kill her, but at least she'd die happy.

"Mmm," he murmured, sliding a finger into her. "You taste so good. Just like I imagined you would."

He'd imagined this? Jesus, even in her wildest fantasies she'd never imagined anything feeling *this* good.

She wanted to scream at him to stop teasing her, to slide into her and fuck her senseless, for God's sake. She wanted to order him to come with her. But words were beyond her. Because right at that moment, as his tongue stroked her, his finger curled up and hit a spot—*the* spot—that had her entire body seizing and clenching as she came harder than she'd ever come before.

And through it all, Nikolai's tongue and fingers kept stroking her, prolonging her orgasm until she was so spent, so thoroughly wrung out, that she could do little more than slump forward, resting her forehead against the wall.

"Oh my God," she said through heavy, panting breaths. "That was…oh my God."

"Yes," he murmured before nipping her shoulder. "And that was only the beginning."

She shivered both in anticipation and at the rough rasp of his voice.

Yep. She wasn't going to survive this.

But what a way to go.

Chapter Twenty-one

Nikolai's heart hammered harder than it ever had before. His senses were overloaded. The sweet, warm scent of her, the sounds of the breathy moans and whimpers that fell from her parted lips, the satin-soft feel of her under his rough fingertips, the incredible taste of her flesh…it was almost too much to take in all at once.

He couldn't wait much longer. He had to have her. Soon.

Violet let out a squeal when he chucked her limp, sated body over his shoulder, stalked into her bedroom, and dumped her on the bed.

In the back of his mind, he knew this was all going too fast. They still had so much to talk through, to work out. He hadn't meant for this to happen tonight.

But she was impossible to resist. And if he was being totally honest with himself, there wasn't really a single fiber of his being left that *wanted* to resist.

And looking down at her now, he had no idea how he'd *ever* been able to keep his hands off her.

Flushed and satisfied, she gazed up at him through lids that were only half open, waiting for him to join her in bed. Waiting for *him*. Nikolai had no idea what he'd done in this life—or a previous life—to deserve her, but he damn sure wasn't going to question it. He supposed he was due for a little luck in his life.

He stripped off his clothes, his movements jerky, as she watched him through lids that were at half-mast.

Nikolai had never really appreciated fine art. But right now? Looking down at Violet's naked body? He had a much better understanding of what inspired artists to paint and sculpt the female form.

Violet was perfectly proportioned. Firm, round breasts just large enough to fill his hands, a waist so tiny he could span it with his hands, gently rounded hips, trim, toned thighs and calves...Jesus, her body wasn't *inspiration* for art, it *was* art.

When she blushed under his scrutiny and moved to cross her arms over her chest, he shook his head. "*Nyet.* Don't you dare hide from me now."

She squirmed on the bed, but didn't try to cover herself again. She reached a hand out to him. "Now. Please."

He briefly wondered if he'd died and gone to heaven. Why else would he be here, with the woman of his dreams laid out before him like an offering from God?

And apparently, he spent too much time wondering, because she shocked the hell out of him by sitting up, grabbing hold of his erection, and dragging him to the edge of the bed so that her face was even with his groin.

He hadn't known what desire really looked like until she

tipped her eyes up to his and wrapped her gorgeous lips around him. He swallowed a shocked gasp when she grabbed one of his hands and guided it to the back of her head, giving him permission to show her exactly how deep he wanted her to take him.

"Jesus Christ, Violet, your mouth is perfection…"

He shivered as the vibration from her answering moan hit him. Need, raw and pure, had him fisting her hair, tangling his fingers in the thick blond strands, but he resisted his body's demand to thrust into her mouth. He wanted her to control this. And besides, there was no way he was going to come in her mouth. When he came, he intended to be balls deep in her tight, wet heat.

But if he didn't stop her soon…

He pulled back, gently tugging on her hair, urging her to let him go. "I'm going to lose control if you keep that up."

The smile that stretched across her wet, shiny lips was full of self-satisfied confidence, and damned if it wasn't the sexiest thing he'd ever seen.

"Maybe I want you to lose control," she said.

He smirked, then dropped to his knees on the mattress between her spread thighs.

"After you," he ordered, leaning down to capture her mouth again.

Chapter Twenty-two

Twenty minutes (or maybe an hour…she wasn't sure) later, Violet didn't think she'd be ever be able to walk again. She couldn't even feel her legs. Her entire body had the strength of a wet Kleenex. She'd come so many times she was pretty sure she was dehydrated.

And Nikolai hadn't even been inside her yet.

"Please," she begged, her voice hoarse from all the screaming and begging she'd done already. "Now."

The smile he gave her as she came down off her fifth orgasm—or maybe it was her sixth? She'd lost count—could only be described as wolfish. "Yes, now I think maybe you're ready."

Violet sent up a silent prayer of thanks to whatever gods might be listening as Nikolai crawled up her body slowly, raking his gaze over every part of her along the way. Given the heat in his eyes, she fully expected him to thrust roughly into her. So, what he did next came as a complete surprise.

He leaned down and gently kissed her nose.

Her heart clenched. She let her fingers trail lightly over a scar on his shoulder, then over the tattoo on his forearm—the one that had branded him as property of Sentry when he was just a child. So much pain and violence in his life, and yet he was still the kind of man who could be so achingly gentle and tender with her.

"Protection?" he asked.

She shook her head. "It's safe. I want to feel you with nothing between us."

That was really all the discussion that was needed. As a *dhampyre*, he was incapable of carrying or transmitting human disease, and she'd been on the pill since she was a teenager.

The thought of making love without a condom was thrilling in and of itself. It was something she'd never even considered doing before. She'd never really felt the need to experience that kind of closeness with another person, or put that much trust in anyone else.

Until now.

Finally, after what felt like an eternity, he slid an arm under her hips and lifted her just enough that he could ease into her, inch by hot, hard, throbbing inch. Her eyes fluttered closed as she reveled in the sensation of him filling her, surrounding her, claiming her as his own. She slid her hands down his back, then grabbed his ass and urged him deeper.

He pulled her leg up and hooked it over his hip as he pressed in deeper. He moaned low in his throat. "You feel amazing."

She arched her back and clutched at his shoulder. "Oh my God, so do you. I…"

He stilled, studying her face as she trailed off. She hoped he couldn't see the blush she felt rising to her cheeks.

She'd almost blurted out that she loved him.

But she couldn't say that now! Not while he was inside her. That was the kind of declaration that was best saved for when level heads prevailed and both parties were fully clothed.

And while she knew that Nikolai had strong feelings for her, he'd never said that he loved her, either. It was just too soon to say those words.

"You what?" he prodded.

Violet bit down on her lower lip and lifted her hips, driving him deeper. He groaned, but obviously recognized a diversion when he saw—or felt—one.

He pulled back until just the tip of his cock was still inside her. His shoulders shook with the effort of his restraint, but he held his ground. "Tell me."

She bit down harder on her lip until she tasted blood. "Please don't stop. I need you." She tightened her thighs around his hips. "I've never needed anyone the way I need you."

He knew that wasn't what she'd intended to say. She could tell by the expression on his face. But apparently her admission—which was also 100% true—was sufficient, because he plunged back into her immediately. "Like this?" he asked, his voice low and throaty.

She whimpered. "God, yes. More."

Nikolai pushed himself up onto his arms, settling his hands on her ribcage. With one last grunt of appreciation as he took in the full view of her body, he started to move, driving into her over and over.

The intense concentration on his face was mesmerizing, but way too controlled for her liking. She wanted him as wild and out of control as she was. She clenched her inner muscles around him.

And that was apparently all it took. His mouth captured hers in a fierce kiss as he surged forward, even deeper than before. She might've cried out, but couldn't be certain. Her entire being was way too focused on him—on the slide of his chest against her breasts with every thrust, on the way his tongue tangled with hers, on the flex and pull of his muscles, rippling under his smooth, taut skin.

It was, by far, the most intense sexual experience Violet had ever had. Every sexual encounter she'd ever had before tonight was vanilla, simple and sweet. But with Nikolai…dark hot chocolate. All. The. Way.

"I'm yours, Violet," he murmured, tracing his tongue over her collarbone. "Always have been. But are you mine?"

Goosebumps broke out all over her body. This was a defining moment. Her brain told her not to engage in any defining moments during sex. Emotions and endorphins were running high, which was just a recipe for bad decision- making. But this was different. This was Nikolai. So, for once in her life, she let her heart answer his question instead of her brain.

"Yes," she whispered, lifting her hips to meet him halfway. "I'm yours."

His breath hitched, but his movements didn't falter. He slipped his arm under her hips again and lifted so he could go deeper, harder.

He rode her slowly, despite her growing desperation and the silent but insistent demand of her hips—*more, harder, faster*—as she ground against him. But when she gave voice to her plea, he moaned her name and grabbed hold of her hips with both hands as he thrust deep, giving her everything she wanted and more until, unbelievably, she came again.

And this time, he came with her, resting his forehead against her collarbone and shuddering in her arms. It was perfect.

He let go of her hips and collapsed on top of her with a deep sigh. Violet had no idea how long they stayed that way, the delicious weight of him pressing her into the mattress, his steady breathing splaying across her neck, his heart beating against hers.

But the longer they stayed silent, the more her brain started nudging her to talk. They needed to talk. He knew it. He'd tried to tell her that before she dragged him off to bed.

"So," she began, trailing her fingers lightly up and down the muscled expanse of his back. "Should we have that talk now?"

He raised his head and smiled down at her, and her breath whooshed out. God, if she could bottle that smile and sell it to lonely, horny women all over the world, she'd never have to work another day in her life.

"Later," he answered. "Much later."

And with that, he pulled out of her, flipped her over onto her knees and slid into her from behind.

Her fingers twisted into the sheets beneath her and she helplessly arched back against him. "Okay," she choked out. "Much later."

Chapter Twenty-three

The next day, Violet sat down at Harper's conference room table, pretending she didn't feel her friend Mischa's eyes on her, taking in her appearance, noting all the little changes she really didn't want to talk about in front of Harper's entire crew.

Mischa sat down right next to her. "You look different," she said.

Violet tucked her hair behind her ear. That morning, before Nikolai dropped her off at Harper's building and he headed out to meet with his PO, she'd tried to take a few moments to pin her hair up as usual. But Nikolai hadn't let her.

Oh, he hadn't forbid her to do it or anything, but when she started working on it, he'd wedged himself between her and the mirror, dropped to his knees, and so thoroughly distracted her with his tongue between her legs that she couldn't remember her own name, let alone how to get her mass of blond curls pinned up into a French twist.

In the end, she arrived right on time for her meeting with Harper. Flushed and slightly disheveled, but right on time. And about as sated as she'd ever been in her life.

Harper sat down across from her and also eyed her critically. "You do look different." Then, she snapped her fingers and said, "Your hair's down!" She gave Violet another once-over, then shrugged. "You look great. But then again, you always look great. No real news there."

"It's not just the hair," Mischa said.

"Where's everyone else?" Violet asked, hoping the change of topic would steer Mischa away from the truth about why she probably looked different this morning.

"Riddick will be here soon," Harper said. "He's dropping Haven off at my mom's house. Lucas and Seven are running down a lead for me, so they won't be here. Benny's on his way, too."

Violet nodded, but could still feel Mischa's eyes boring into the side of her head. After a few more tense moments, Mischa blurted out, "You had sex!"

Violet sucked in an outraged gasp. "You *promised* you'd never read my mind without my permission!"

Mischa threw her hands up in the universal sign of surrender. "I didn't! I can tell just by looking at you. You're all relaxed and happy-looking."

Harper grinned at her. "It was Comrade Hottie, wasn't it?" When Violet didn't answer, Harper's smile melted into a grimace. "Please tell me it was the hot Russian and not the twatwaffle with the comb-over."

Just the thought of sex with Miles made her shiver. And *not* in the fun way. "I haven't seen Miles since I broke up with him." There'd been some increasingly odd and desperate-sounding messages on her voice mail from him, but she'd started deleting those without even bothering to listen to them. He'd give up and accept that they were finished sooner or later. Calling him back would only offer him false hope. "And my sex life really isn't any of your business." She stabbed a finger at Mischa. "You better not try to read my mind, either!"

"I wouldn't," Mischa said, indignant. "I'd never violate your privacy like that."

Harper rolled her eyes. "Ugh. You're such a Girl Scout. I'd *totally* violate her privacy like that. In fact…"

Violet squealed as Harper latched onto her wrist with a freaking Kung Fu grip. She tried to pull away, but Harper was freakishly strong for such a tiny woman—and she was obviously accustomed to holding onto people who wanted to escape her and her visions, because her hold was like a manacle.

After a moment—when the vision subsided, Violet assumed—Harper let go of Violet and slumped back in her chair. She fanned her cheeks, which were now flaming red. God only knows how much she'd seen of what Violet and Nikolai had done the previous night.

"Wow," Harper said on a gusty sigh. "That was…wow. I think I need a cigarette."

"You don't smoke," Mischa said.

Harper fanned her face some more. "I might start after that. Way to go, Vi! I'm proud of you. When you let loose, you *really* let loose."

Harper glanced at Mischa, held her hands apart about ten inches and mouthed, "His dick is huge!"

Mischa let out a laugh/cough combo that kind of sounded like a barking seal before clearing her throat and offering Violet a sympathetic, mumbled, "Sorry."

Violet was stuck in emotional limbo somewhere between embarrassed by what Harper had seen, furious about the invasion of privacy, and confused as to how this conversation had even started at all. In the end, all she was able to do was grumble, while pointing accusingly at Harper, "You're horrible."

Harper nodded, looking vaguely apologetic. But only vaguely. "Yeah," she admitted with a shrug. "I get that a lot."

Riddick chose to make an appearance at that point, mumbling a half-hearted greeting to Violet and Mischa, and once again giving his wife a kiss like he'd been off to war and hadn't seen her for the past five years.

When he finally took his seat next to Harper, she didn't even bother to whisper when she said, "You. Me. Naked. As soon this meeting is over, yeah?"

His grin was answer enough.

Benny came skidding in—disheveled and frantic looking—like Kramer in *Seinfeld*. He threw himself into a chair on the other side of Violet and blew out a deep sigh. "Sorry I'm late, guys. I was with Angela. You wouldn't *believe* what she suggested we do this morning—"

Mischa held up her hand. "I'm going to have to stop you there, Benny."

"But I—"

"No, I wasn't kidding. If you continue with that sentence, I'm going to *have to stop you*."

It was clear from her tone that "stop you" implied violence of some sort. Violet wasn't usually onboard for violence, but in this case, it was probably warranted.

Mischa narrowed her eyes on him until he gulped and said, "Yeah, yeah. I get it. It wasn't nothing important anyhow."

Then he glanced at Violet and tipped his head to one side like a confused puppy. "You look different."

And just like when she'd punched Darren in the face at her sister's wedding, Violet felt something in her brain snap, and she blurted, "I had sex, alright? Lots and lots of hot, dirty, wet, thrusting, *sex* in every room of my apartment, OK? I almost couldn't walk this morning because, yes, Harper, *it's huge*, alright? Is *that* what you all wanted to hear? Huh? Is *that* good enough for you all?"

Benny blinked owlishly at her. "I was gonna say that your hair looks nice like that is all," he said in a small voice.

She glanced over at Riddick, who held up his hands in surrender and said, "Hey, I don't have a dog in the race. I couldn't possibly care less who you're banging. But if it helps, the Russian is probably a step up from the accountant."

"Actuary," Mischa corrected.

Riddick grimaced. "Like that's any better."

In her head, Violet was screaming. But she was guessing that screaming at this particular crew wouldn't do her any good, so instead, she let her forehead drop to the conference room table with a *thunk*.

Mischa rubbed a hand up and down Violet's back soothingly. "Oh, don't worry about it. Good sex is nothing to be ashamed of. It was good, right?"

"Yes," Harper answered.

Violet lifted her head and glared at her.

Harper almost sounded sincere when she apologized that time.

"Yes, it was…" *Mind-blowing? Earth-shattering? Everything I never knew I needed in my life?* "…good. But can we change the topic, please? I'm not exactly comfortable talking about my sex life in a business meeting."

"Oh, come on," Harper whined. "Don't be such a poop."

Riddick laid his hand over his wife's on the table. "Please, babe. For the love of God, let her be a poop, because as much as she doesn't want to *talk* about her sex life, I don't want to *hear* about it."

"Fine," Harper said on a gusty sigh. "Be a lady-boner killer. I'm still happy for you, Vi, even if you are absolutely zero fun."

Violet was happy for herself, too. She was just also in a perpetual state of panic, wondering when this newfound joy was going to be ripped away from her. She hated to be negative, but…well, what proof did she really have that things in her life could go any way *but* negative?

"Why don't you tell her where her case stands?" Mischa suggested.

Harper sat up straighter and folded her hands together, obviously shifting from curious, intrusive friend mode into *professional detective* mode. "Well, as part of the investigation, Hunter provided us with information on all of your paranormal patients." When Violet's spine stiffened, Harper hastened to add, "Nothing that would violate their patient rights. Just some general questions about their whereabouts during the times when you were shot at, and when your apartment was vandalized. Your name was never mentioned in any of the conversations. We just said there'd been some crime in their neighborhoods during those times, and that we were just trying to find anyone who'd seen anything."

She relaxed a bit. She hated the idea of her patients thinking she suspected them of any wrongdoing. Even if they were, well, *totally* capable of wrongdoing, that'd be a huge blow to the trust they put in her as a therapist. "And did they all check out?"

"I think *check out*," Harper said, making finger quotes, "would be a gross overstatement. Right, Benny?"

Benny shook his head, his expression somewhere between amused and horrified. "Dude, your patients are fucked *up*."

He didn't know the half of it. "Maybe, but are any of them trying to kill me?"

Benny shook his head. "Nah. They all had good alibis for the times in question. Except for one dude, and judging by how I had to talk to him through the peephole in his front door next to a pile of rotting mail that looked like it hadn't been taken in for the past decade or so, I'm guessing he's not our man, either."

Mr. Alvarez, Violet knew. An agoraphobia sufferer who hadn't left his home since vampires were outed. He was sure that if he left his home, he'd be met with a pitchfork mob waiting to burn him alive. And since that exact same thing happened to him back in Salem in 1692, when he'd been accused of witchcraft, Violet couldn't really say she blamed him.

But Mr. Alvarez was a good guy. He'd never expressed anything other than gratitude towards her, and had always been very appreciative of her for agreeing to handle their sessions through video conferencing. And he was making good progress. She imagined she'd eventually even be able to convince him to leave his home if he kept up with his sessions. He had no motive to try to kill her, nor did he have the access to the outside world required to kill her.

It was both a blessing and a curse to realize that none of her patients were suspects. One the one hand, her patients weren't trying to kill her, so…woo hoo! But on the other hand, it would be a huge relief to have at least one viable suspect.

"Hunter also checked out vampires the Council had previous problems with," Harper went on. "And by *problems*, we of course mean anyone who was likely to go all murder-y and rage-y for no apparent reason. Unfortunately, he came up empty on that front, too."

Well…hell. "So, what now?"

Harper leaned forward, resting her elbows on the table. "Like I said, I've got Seven and Lucas running down one last lead. I'll tell you about it if they find anything. But for right now, I don't want you to worry about it, OK?"

She swallowed hard. It was kind of hard not to worry at the moment. Thank God she had Nikolai watching her back. And her front. And pretty much every part of her after last night.

Harper smirked at her. "Flashbacks, huh? The flushed cheeks are a dead giveaway."

Benny chuckled. "Yeah, you look like you just got a *Silkwood* shower."

When everyone stared blankly at him, he hastened to add, "You know, *Silkwood*. Meryl Streep? Cher? Working in the power plant and getting cooked by radiation? They'd put 'em in the shower and scrub their skin off to get rid of it?"

One loaded pause later, he grumbled, "Oh, never mind. You kids today just got no culture."

"Anyhoo," Harper said after another long beat. "Vi, I need you to stick close to Nikolai. Now that we've exhausted our legal means of investigating this thing, we're going to go on the dark net for the paranormal community and see if we can pick up any chatter about who might have it in for you."

Violet blinked, nonplussed. "There's a dark net for the paranormal community?"

"There's a dark net for everything," Mischa said. Then she cracked her knuckles and added, "But no one can hide from me. If they've left a cyber trail, I can find it."

Of that Violet had no doubt. There was a reason Mischa was the official enforcer for the vampire council. Well, several, really.

First of all, Mischa was the second most powerful vampire in the country, possibly even the world. Second of all, she was a certified genius, and her years as a watcher with Sentry had given her problem-solving and tracking skills few people in the world could match. And finally, when she went after something or someone, Mischa was a relentless bitch who wouldn't stop until she got exactly what she wanted.

And who didn't want to be friends with a relentless bitch who'd hack the paranormal dark net and track down a would-be killer for her?

"Of course, if that doesn't work, you could make yourself bait and wander around town after dark, hoping someone will take a shot at you," Riddick said in a tone so dry it made Violet crave a tall glass of ice water just contemplating it.

Harper turned a dark scowl on her husband. "One time. It was *one time* that I played bait to lure out a serial killer, and you're just never going to let it go, are you?"

Riddick didn't even flinch like Violet would've under the power of Harper's scowl as he crossed his arms over his chest and said, "No."

"And it worked," Harper grumbled. "But you always leave

that part out."

"If by *work*," he said, making finger quotes, "you mean you flushed him out of hiding and ended up chained to his basement floor, well, then, *sure*, I guess it technically *worked*."

Harper rolled her eyes and waved a hand dismissively. "Po-ta-toe, po-tah-toe. Whatever. The point is, I'm here and he isn't. So, I win."

Benny frowned. "What does that even mean, anyway? Does anyone really say po-tah-toe? I never understood that saying."

"It doesn't matter," Mischa said. "She'd use any argument to claim a victory, no matter how stupid it sounds. I don't even know why he'd ever disagree with her to begin with."

"Good point," Riddick mumbled.

Harper snorted. "About time you see things my way. I was getting ready to cancel sexy naked fun time."

He raised a brow at her.

She sighed. "OK, so that's not true. But it totally *could've* been true. You're not irresistible to me, you know!"

The brow went a little higher until Harper groaned and said, "Fine. You're irresistible to me, but it's still rude to throw past *questionable* decisions up in my face."

"That's as close as you'll ever get to an admission of wrongdoing," Mischa told Riddick. "I'd take it if I were you."

He kept his eyes trained on his wife as he said, "Oh, I intend to take it, all right."

The dirty emphasis he put on the word "take" had Harper's cheeks pinking up in a way that told Violet sexy naked fun time had never really been off the table and they both knew it.

God, what it must be like to have someone in your life that supported and wanted you no matter what. Someone who knew the real you and overlooked—celebrated, even—your every foible and flaw. Someone who…

"Oh, my God!" Violet cried out, causing Benny to spill his coffee all over his shirt.

"Jesus, doc," he grumbled, grabbing a handful of napkins off the table to mop up the mess on his T-shirt. "What the fuck?"

When she'd almost blurted out that she loved Nikolai yesterday, she'd really meant it! It hadn't been a sexual thing at all. And who was she to judge how soon was *too soon* to love someone? There was no reason in hell to make him say it first, either. What a stupid, old-fashioned notion. She'd been an idiot not to tell him how she'd felt in that moment.

Then, a horrifying thought occurred to her. They never really got around to talking more. What if he thought last night had been about nothing but sex for her? Just scratching her itch?

"I have to go," Violet blurted. "Right now. I need someone to take me to Nikolai. Right now."

Riddick, Mischa, and Benny looked confused, but after a moment of loaded silence, Harper grinned at her. "Oh, *I* know that look." She gestured to Violet's face. "You have epiphany face." Then, to Riddick, she smugly added, "There's a certain hot Russian who's about to have his happy ending."

Riddick grimaced. "Did I mention I *really* don't want to hear about Violet's sex life?"

Harper elbowed him in the gut. "Not *that* kind of happy ending. I'm talking about the big love declaration."

He frowned as if thinking about it, then said, "No, I don't really want to hear about that, either."

Mischa rolled her eyes. "Ugh. Forget these dumbasses, Vi. I'll take you to Nikolai. Don't worry about it."

Harper made a rude noise. "No fucking way. I wanna see the love declaration. We're all going."

Benny stopped wiping at the coffee on his shirt and stood up. "Yeah, I'm in. I love a good love declaration."

"I still don't give a fuck," Riddick said with a shrug. "But I go where Harper goes."

Harper clapped her hands together. "Great! Then we're all in agreement." She glanced at her watch. "I've only got a few hours before I have to pick up the munchkin at my mom's, so let's hit the road."

Any other day, Violet would be mortified at the thought of showing up to tell a man she loved him with an audience. Especially *this* audience. But today? The only thing that mattered was getting to Nikolai and telling him what she should have told him last night—what she'd been too damn blind to see until this moment.

"Fine," Violet said through gritted teeth. "But we take the fastest car with the fastest driver."

Harper's grin was way too innocent for Violet's liking. "I guess that'd be me."

Chapter Twenty-four

Nikolai was just stepping out of his PO's office when Seven's voice stopped him.

"Meeting up with your babysitter?" she asked with a grin.

He grimaced. He'd never enjoy hearing that word, even though it seemed to give Seven *great* joy to say it. But, he was in far too good a mood today—and way too anxious to get back to Violet, if he was being honest with himself—to argue with anyone.

"You could say that," he answered. "What about you? What are you doing here?"

She pointed to the building next door to his PO's brownstone. "Checking on a lead for Harper. I won't know for sure until Lucas checks things out at the station, but I have a good idea who Violet's stalker is."

Which was good, but once her stalker was found, Violet wouldn't need him anymore. Would she even still *want* him? Last night made him think she would, but how could he be sure? He clearly felt a lot more for her than she felt for him. And who could blame her, really? With his past, with the way he was…being with him wouldn't be easy. Would Violet be able to tolerate him for the long-haul?

"Seven, can I ask you something?"

She shrugged. "Sure." Then as she thought for a moment, she looked nervous and added, "Unless you're sad about something. I'm not very good at offering comfort. But I can call Harper if—"

Nikolai shuddered at the thought of ever being in sorry enough shape that he needed comfort from Harper Hall. "No, I'm not sad. I was just wondering…has it been…" Jesus, why was this so hard to explain? Seemed liked the right words were always just outside his reach. "…*hard* for you to adjust to life outside of Sentry? With normal people, I mean?"

"Am I *ever* with normal people?"

Touché. "I mean, how do you go about…"

Seven laid a hand on his shoulder. "Look, Nikolai, it's me you're talking to. You don't have to beat around the bush. You know I won't be offended by anything you want to ask like Mischa would be, and I won't turn everything you say into a comedy bit like Harper and Benny would. You can say anything to me, OK?"

Well, you asked for it, he thought before he blurted, "How did you get Lucas to fall in love with you?"

A frown line creased her brow as she thought about the question. "I don't know that I really *did* anything in particular to make him fall in love with me. He just *did*."

Probably not a good comparison, he thought. Seven was beautiful and sweet-natured, despite her past with Sentry. She was loveable. Nikolai was, well, more *complicated* than that. "Forget I asked," he said, struggling for a careless tone. "It's not important."

Her frown deepened. "Well, yes it is, because you just lied to me. I heard your breathing and heart rate increase."

He sighed. "It's not really a *lie*. It *shouldn't* be important."

"But it is. This is about Violet, isn't it?"

Maybe he hadn't done such a shit job communicating after all. Or, more likely, Seven was more perceptive than he'd given her credit for. He rubbed a hand over the back of his neck. "Yes. I'm just…"

She nodded when he trailed off. "I know this face you're making. You're feeling bad about your past and things you did when you were with Sentry, and you're wondering how someone like Violet could ever really love you, right?"

"Well…yes," he answered.

Sure, she'd given him access to her body, but could she ever give him her heart as easily? He just couldn't see it happening.

"So, you're kind of feeling sorry for yourself, right?"

Wow, he thought, she'd been right. She really *wasn't* any good at offering comfort. "Seven, I'm hopelessly in love with the woman of my dreams and I have no idea what she feels for me, or even if she *could* ever feel anything for me other than lust. So, yes, I think it's safe to say I'm feeling a little sorry for myself."

Seven seemed to have completely missed his decidedly grumpy tone, because she merely nodded again and said, "Sometimes I feel sorry for myself, too. Not often, but every now and then, I feel bad about my childhood, or about something I did when I was with Sentry, and I wonder if I really deserve all the good things I have in my life right now. And you know what? Harper's sister Marina said something to me one time that really helped."

Shit, he was almost afraid to ask. "What was it?"

"She said, 'Suck it up, buttercup! You've got great hair, a perfect ass, and you've gotten laid recently—so from where I'm standing, you ain't got it so bad! Quit bellyaching about your problems and worry about someone who *really* has it bad, heh?'"

Nikolai wasn't sure if it was the words, or Seven's spot-on mimic of Marina's thick New York accent that struck him temporarily dumb and mute. But after he just stared at her for a few unblinking moments, she shrugged and added, "I figured since all that applied to you, too, it might be helpful."

He finally found his voice and said, "Um...thank you?"

She slapped him in the shoulder hard enough to nearly topple him. "You're welcome."

It was in that moment he decided he'd just have to talk to Violet. Ask her how she felt. And if she didn't love him the way he loved her, he'd just have to do whatever he could to change her mind. Make her see that he wasn't going anywhere, even after her case was put to rest. He'd do whatever he could to…

The violent, incessant blare of a car horn jerked him from his musings. A blue Mustang screeched to a stop at the curb just a few feet from where Nikolai and Seven were chatting.

Nikolai recognized the car before the driver threw her door open and hopped out. After all, you never really forgot the first trunk you'd ever been stuffed into.

Harper waved and leaned into the car to flip the driver's seat up so that Riddick, Benny and Mischa—Jesus, how had they all fit back there? It looked like they were shuffling out of a clown car—could climb out of the back seat. "Hi, guys! Comrade, this is your lucky day."

Nikolai sighed. He'd probably never be able to convince her to stop calling him that, so why bother trying? Then Violet got out of the passenger seat and he quit caring about Harper and her silly nicknames for him.

Her eyes locked with his and relief smoothed out the lines of tension around her beautiful mouth. She looked troubled. Had she gotten another death threat? He was pretty much done waiting for Harper to solve the case. He'd just have to hunt the bastard down himself. And when he found him, that son of a bitch would *beg* for a quick death.

But that and pretty much every other thought in his head evaporated when Violet ran up and threw herself at him, wrapping her arms around him tight enough to make sucking in a deep breath impossible. Not that it mattered. If given the choice between air and Violet in his arms, he'd choose Violet every time.

Nikolai wrapped his arms around her and she sighed as she tucked her face into the spot where his neck and shoulder met. It was as if the spot had been crafted specifically for her.

"What's the matter, *kotehok*? Did something happen? Your stalker?"

She tightened her grip on him. "No. I just had to talk to you."

Nikolai had next to nothing in the way of experience with relationships, but from what he'd heard, when a woman wanted to talk to you and went out of her way to track you down, chances were you wouldn't like what she had to say.

"Alright," he said cautiously. "You can tell me anything."

Even if all you need to tell me is that you don't want me around anymore. It'll feel about like having my heart ripped out, stomped into the dirt, and then thrown back in my face, but, sure, go ahead and tell me anything.

She took a deep breath and looked up at him. "I started to say something to you last night, but I didn't let myself finish because…well, I was a coward, I guess. But today I'm not."

He swallowed hard. "And?"

"And—"

"Nikolai Aleyev."

Nikolai looked over the top of Violet's head at the man who'd just shouldered past Mischa and Harper on the sidewalk to get to him. He squinted at him until recognition hit. "Detective Cunningham, yes?"

Cunningham nodded and hitched up his sagging pants. "I'm going to need you to come down to the station with me and answer a few questions."

Violet didn't let go of him, but glanced at Cunningham over her shoulder. "Is this about my case, Officer?"

"Yes, ma'am. It turns out there were several other homes vandalized in your neighborhood around the time of your break-in. We have an eyewitness who saw a man matching your description, Mr. Aleyev, fleeing one of those crime scenes."

Violet sputtered. "You can't be serious! You think *Nikolai* had something to do with my break-in? You think the man who's been protecting me day and night might be the one who broke into my home and left me a death threat?"

Harper snorted. "You're reaching so far on this one, Cunningham, you're gonna throw your back out."

The officer scowled at her. "I don't recall asking for your opinion, Hall."

She shrugged. "That's never really stopped me before."

Mischa stepped forward, hands on hips. "Cunningham, this man is a *dhampyre*. You know that. He has rights that are protected by the Council." Her eyes narrowed on him. "And in case you've forgotten, *I* am part of the Council."

Cunningham gulped, but held his ground. "Of course I know that. We're not arresting Mr. Aleyev."

Yet, Nikolai thought. Cunningham didn't say it, but he heard it nonetheless. They had exactly one suspect at this point, and they intended to focus all their energy on proving his guilt. The human police in this town didn't seem to look any further in front of them than the nearest vampire or *dhampyre* when crimes were unsolved for a certain amount of time.

"We just want to ask him a few questions," Cunningham added. Then he smirked at Mischa and said, "Which I'm sure *you* know is perfectly within my rights as a lowly human public servant."

Riddick snagged Mischa's arm when she swayed forward, looking ready to rip into Cunningham, but he wasn't able to stop her from hissing at the cop. The power she exuded with that one menacing hiss raised the tiny hairs on the back of Nikolai's neck. If Cunningham knew what was good for him, he'd run. Mischa could probably kill the dumb bastard without laying a finger on him.

"Adouchenozzlesayswhat?" Benny asked Cunningham.

Cunningham frowned at him, confused. "What?"

Benny and Harper snickered, then fist-bumped like a couple of teenagers. Riddick face-palmed, and Mischa ignored them, keeping her narrow-eyed focus on Cunningham. "You can't force him to do anything," she said in a low, scary voice.

But Cunningham was either brave or stupid, because he lifted his chin and spat back, "I can have a chat with his PO. Jam him up pretty good if I want to. Could make it pretty hard for him to keep a job if the cops are always keeping an eye on him, wanting to question him. And you know that not being able to keep a job violates his parole." He narrowed his eyes on Mischa. "Your better half wouldn't have a choice but to force him to serve out his suspended sentence at Midvale."

Well, that's it, Nikolai thought. Mischa was going to annihilate this hapless little fuck. But it wasn't Mischa who stepped between him and Cunningham. It was Seven.

Seven stood toe-to-toe with Cunningham, hands on her hips. And even though she was a good five inches shorter and a hundred pounds lighter, the cop paled a bit under the intensity of her stare. "Threatening my friend would be a mistake. The last you'd ever make."

Cunningham hitched up his pants again and glared down at her. "Move, little girl, or I'll move you."

The smile Seven gave him was nothing short of bone-chilling. "I dare you," she whispered.

Her tone left no doubt in Nikolai's mind that if he needed her to, Seven would kill this man, disappear his corpse, and never speak of it again. But she wasn't a killer anymore. She had a family and love and a real life. So did Mischa. There was no way he was going to let either of them sacrifice anything on his behalf.

While Cunningham visibly groped for a reply, Nikolai laid a hand on Seven's shoulder and gave her a gentle shove into her brother's arms before saying to Cunningham, "I'll go with you and answer your questions."

In his arms, Violet trembled, and he tightened his hold on her for a moment. She probably thought he was going to end up in Midvale when this was all done. She'd been instrumental in getting Seven out of Midvale, so she knew better than anyone what a hellhole it was. Roaches had better living conditions than the prisoners there.

He kissed the top of her head and tipped her chin up so that she was forced to look him in the eye. "Stay close to Harper or Riddick until I get back, yes?"

"Hey, what am I, chopped liver?" Benny muttered. "I've been

known to kick ass a time or two myself, you know."

Violet's lower lip trembled, and he couldn't stop himself capturing her mouth in a quick, hard kiss.

Cunningham grabbed his upper arm. "Come on, Casanova. Time to go."

He offered Violet what he hoped was a reassuring smile. "We'll talk tonight."

She opened her mouth, looking like she was going to argue, but Riddick grabbed her arm and pulled her toward him so that she was on his left side, Seven on his right. He gave Nikolai a nod, which Nikolai took to mean that Violet was safe in his care for the time being.

"I'm calling Hunter," Mischa grumbled. "I'm having him send a Council lawyer over right away."

Cunningham rolled his eyes as he led Nikolai to his unmarked cruiser. "Yeah, you do that, girlie."

This time it was Harper and Benny who grabbed Mischa's arms and held her back when she lunged at the cop. But Nikolai ignored the creative threats she hurled at Cunningham. He held eye contact with Violet the whole time he was walked to the car and shoved into the back seat, telling her without words that everything was going to be fine.

Even though he wasn't entirely sure it would.

When the car pulled away from the curb, as Violet's entire body shook from the rush of anger and fear and the sheer *injustice* of it all, Harper sighed and said, "Well, *that* didn't go at all as planned, did it?"

Violet couldn't hold back a derisive snort. "You think?"

Harper just shook her head. "The big love declarations just aren't as simple as the Hallmark Channel would lead us to believe."

"Word," Benny agreed.

Yes. Word indeed.

Chapter Twenty-five

Two hours and three cups of crappy police station coffee later, and Cunningham *still* hadn't released Nikolai. Violet was starting to wonder if he ever would. Maybe they just planned to keep him in that interrogation room, grilling him until he confessed to something, *anything* they could officially lock him up for.

Harper didn't look up from her phone, but said, "If you don't sit down willingly, I'm going to *sit* you down. I'll super glue your ass to that chair if I have to. Your pacing isn't doing anyone any good, and it's driving me nuts."

With a heavy sigh and absolutely zero doubt that Harper would make good on her threat, Violet dropped into the hard plastic chair next to Harper. They were sitting in the middle of the police station's bullpen, and the combined smell of day-old doughnuts, burnt coffee, dust, and something unidentifiable (the stench of injustice, most likely) were starting to give Violet a headache.

Or maybe that was just the lingering possibility of Nikolai being sent to Midvale for crimes he didn't commit that was paining her so.

Harper slipped her phone back into her oversized, slouchy handbag and glanced over at Violet. "It's going to be OK, you know. The lawyer Hunter sent over is the best. He's a total weasel—figuratively and literally, since he's a weasel shifter—but really good at what he does. Trust me. When he's done with them, the cops will be tripping all over themselves to apologize to Nikolai and fist-fighting over who gets to drive him home."

God, Violet hoped Harper was right. Nikolai had already been through so much. He deserved for things to go his way just this once. Then, the other part of what Harper said sank in, and she asked, "There are weasel shifters?"

Across from them, sprawled across a lumpy brown leather loveseat reading what looked to be a year-old copy of *Guns and Ammo* magazine he'd lifted from a cop's desk drawer, Benny snorted and said, "Doc, there are *every* kind of shifters out there. There was this dude who used to come into the Rag Tag every month." He held his hand up. "Hand to Jesus, alpaca shifter."

Harper leaned forward in her chair. "Really?"

"I shit you not. And don't even get me started on the honey badger shifters." He shuddered.

"Oh, I have *so* many questions."

Violet tuned them out as Harper fired her alpaca and honey badger shifter questions at Benny. Not that she wasn't grateful for the distraction from what must be going on in the interrogation room with Nikolai, but she almost wished Harper and Benny had left with Mischa and Riddick. Some alone time definitely would be welcome at the moment. Time to figure out exactly what she was going to say to Nikolai when he finally—

Violet gasped as the power went out. The harsh overhead fluorescent lights, computers, desktop fans, the whir of the heating and air conditioning system…it all died, leaving an eerie stillness in its wake, an utter lack of sound that was almost unheard of in the city.

The handful of cops that were scattered around the bullpen started murmuring, wondering when the backup generator was going to kick in and power everything back up.

It didn't.

Harper made a noise that was half growl, half groan. "Swear to God, if Mischa and Hunter are fucking and knocked the power out again, I'm gonna be pissed."

Violet glanced toward the only window in the room and saw the faint, blinking neon-pink glow of the Jack's Doughnuts sign next door. A growing sense of dread gnawed at her. "It's not a city-wide blackout."

"Oh, man," Benny whispered. "I do *not* have a good feeling about this."

Harper eased a Glock out of her purse and the sound it made as she pulled back the slide and let it spring forward was as loud as cannon fire in the quiet station. "I don't either," she muttered.

The front door of the station made a sound like a wail of pain as it screeched open on rusty hinges. The cop closest to the door had only a scant second to yell, "Gun!" before a shot was fired.

"Get down!" Harper shouted, shoving Violet to the floor.

Two more shots were fired as Benny dove on top of her, shielding her with his body as the cops around them rushed the shooter. Or, *shooters*, more likely, as it now sounded.

Screams and the frantic shouting of orders filled the air as shots were fired and bullets pinged off the walls around them, but Violet could barely hear them over her own ragged breathing and the pounding of her pulse.

Above her, Benny's body flinched, then was suddenly just…gone. As if he'd been lifted and thrown off her. Before Violet could even think of getting away, something sharp pinched her neck.

She heard Harper scream her name and fire off a shot before everything went black.

Chapter Twenty-six

Nikolai was pretty sure his heart stopped when the lights went out and the gunfire started.

Violet.

He shot to his feet, giving the cuffs they'd used to chain him to the interrogation table—*standard procedure, my ass*—a tug. The cuffs remained intact, but the table lifted a good inch or two off the ground. Great. He really didn't want to have to drag the fucking table around with him, but he supposed he could if necessary. "You need to let me go. Now."

Cunningham crouched down behind the door, gun drawn and poised to shoot at anyone who might try to get into the room. The lawyer had dived under the table when the first shot was fired.

"Get down, dumbass!" Cunningham shouted at Nikolai. "You're going to get yourself shot."

Screams, pained grunts, and more gunfire sounded on the other side of the door. Nikolai's head spun. It sounded like the end of the world out there and Violet was right in the middle of all of it.

"Please," he spit out, not even caring how desperate he sounded. "I have to get to her! You have to let me go!"

"You're not going anywhere," Cunningham spit back at him. "How do I know you're not behind all this and those aren't your people out there?"

Jesus. He'd been a damn fool to think he could explain anything to this guy, to prove his innocence or his devotion to Violet. In this cop's small mind, Nikolai was the bad guy and always would be.

He'd tried to do this the right way. The human way. And look where it'd gotten him. Chained to a desk in a police station under siege while the woman he loved was right on the other side of the door, probably fearing for her life.

Time to do things the only way he knew for a fact worked.

Adrenaline flooded his system as he leapt onto the table, holding it down with his weight while he yanked on the cuffs with all his strength. The cuffs snapped under the pressure.

Cunningham turned, his eyes widening as he instinctively turned his gun on Nikolai. In a flash of inhuman speed, he jumped down and rushed Cunningham, snatching the gun from his hand and flinging it across the room before shoving the cop out of his way. His elbow hit the cop's nose in the process and blood splattered across the front of Nikolai's shirt.

"Ow, Jesus, you broke my fucking nose!" Cunningham wailed from his position on the floor. He tried to get up, but Nikolai shoved him back down.

"Stay down," he ordered.

"You're going to rot in Midvale, motherfucker!" Cunningham cried, pressing a hand over his bloody nose. "You'll pay for this!"

"You can't threaten my client like that!" the lawyer shouted from his hiding spot under the table. "The Council will see to it that you're—"

Nikolai ignored them both as he eased the door open and stepped into the darkened bullpen. The acrid stench of gunpowder burned his nostrils as he scanned the room. Fortunately, *dhampyres* had superior night vision, so the power outage didn't really slow him down.

Son of a bitch, the place was crawling with hostiles, all vampires, all armed. The human cops were hopelessly outmanned. Half of the ones who'd been in the bullpen when Nikolai went into the interrogation room were down, wounded or dead. The other half were gone, having either left before the shooting started, or run when it did.

And he didn't see Violet anywhere.

He'd just have to kill every last one of these motherfuckers until he found her. Might as well start right *here*...

Nikolai grabbed the gun hand of the vampire closest to him, aimed it at one of the other's heads, double-tapped the trigger, then snapped the vamp's neck before he even had time to react. The two limp bodies hit the floor at the same moment, but Nikolai had already moved on to his next target.

A monster of a vamp in some kind of biker club cut had a wounded cop down on the ground and was trying to feed off him. The cop was kicking and clawing at the vamp, but with what looked to be a gunshot wound through his shoulder, his efforts were ineffectual at best.

Nikolai grabbed a fistful of the biker vamp's greasy ponytail and yanked him off the cop, tossing him backward. Then he caught the vamp with a back-kick to the chin. The sound of crunching bone and cartilage let him know the vamp's neck had snapped on impact, but once again, before the vamp's body hit the floor, Nikolai moved on.

Two vamps came at him at once and before he could drop into his fighting stance, Riddick popped up behind the vamps, grabbed their heads, and smashed their skulls together. When they dropped to the ground, he gave each a swift kick to the head—for good measure or for his own enjoyment, Nikolai wasn't sure.

"Where the fuck is my wife?" Riddick growled at Nikolai.

"I don't know. Where the fuck is Violet?" he growled right back.

"Riddick, I'm here."

Riddick swung around and his gaze shot straight to his wife. And then to the vampire who held her against his chest like a human shield with a knife to her throat. "Let her go," he ordered.

The menace behind those words, spoken in that rough, feral voice, would've given Nikolai pause. Would've made him consider letting the woman go if he'd been in this vampire's position. But the vamp was obviously too stupid to recognize he was prey in this scenario. Riddick was clearly the predator.

While the vamp was focused on Riddick, Nikolai reached down and pried a Glock out of a dead cop's hand. He aimed it at the vampire's head, but he didn't have a clean shot. Not with Harper right in front of him like that.

"Let her go *or what?*" the vampire sneered at Riddick. "What will you do?"

Riddick shrugged in a gesture that would've looked careless to anyone who couldn't feel the waves of rage and menace rolling off him. "I won't have to do anything. If you don't let her go, she'll fuck you up."

The vampire chuckled. "Is that right?"

Riddick nodded and shifted his gaze back to his wife. "Isn't that right, baby?"

"Fuckin-A, that's right," Harper growled.

And with that, Harper stomped down hard on the vampire's instep. When he loosened his hold on her, she drove her elbow back, knocking the knife from his grip. Then, for apparently no other reason than she was good and pissed off, she reached down, grabbed a handful of the dumb bastard's nuts, and twisted with everything she had.

The vampire promptly puked, dropped to the ground like a sack of wet shit, and curled into the fetal position, mouth gaping in a silent scream.

Riddick grabbed Harper and tugged her roughly into his arms.

"Jesus," he muttered, stroking his wife's hair as he held her against his chest. "I heard the station was being attacked over the police scanner. I was fucking terrified. What the fuck happened?"

"I don't have any idea what happened," Harper said, her voice slightly shaky and muffled against Riddick's chest. "One minute everything was fine, and the next, the place was crawling with vampires shooting at anything human that moved. The one that grabbed me and one other one were specifically looking for Violet."

Nikolai took aim at the vampire's head once again, but Harper stopped him. "Don't," she said, her voice muffled against Riddick's chest. "We might need to get answers from him."

The lights came back on at that moment and Nikolai blinked several times to clear his vision, then he took in the carnage around them.

Jesus, what a mess.

"Oh, my God!" Harper cried, shoving away from Riddick. "Benny!"

The halfer was curled up on the ground, arms curved protectively over his head. The blood stains and rips on the back of his shirt suggested he'd been caught by a couple of—wait, no, *three*—stray bullets.

Harper dropped to her knees and slid her arms under Benny, clutching him tightly to her chest. "Wake up, damn it!" she shouted at him. "Don't you dare die on me, motherfucker!"

Benny let out a low moan, followed by a dry, hacking cough. Harper let out a relieved sigh and loosened her grip until Benny's head was resting in her lap. "Oh my God," she muttered. "Thank you, Jesus."

Benny blinked, then squinted up at her. "Am I dead? Is this heaven?"

Harper grinned down at him, tears shining in her eyes. "We're in a smelly police station, Benny. Why would you think this is heaven?"

He coughed again, then said, "'Cause I woke up with my face pressed into your boobs, and you was talking about God and Jesus. Figured I must be dead, 'cause why else would I be feeling your boobs on my face? But I ain't dead?"

"No, but you will be if you ever think about or mention my wife's boobs again," Riddick warned dryly.

Harper ran her hands over his shirt. "Your vampire blood will heal you, as long as the bullets are out. It'll just take some time."

Time—and patience—was something Nikolai was just fresh out of at the moment. "Where the fuck is Violet?"

Benny lifted his head off Harper's lap, wincing as he rolled his head around on his neck. "When the shooting started, Harper pushed her down and I covered her. But the guy who shot me…I'm pretty sure he grabbed her right before I passed out. I'm so sorry, man. There wasn't nothin' I could do."

Nikolai shoved a hand through his hair, fighting for the cool detachment that had gotten him through so many missions for Sentry. Him panicking wouldn't do Violet a damn bit of good. She needed him to stay sharp, focused.

"It's not your fault," Harper said to Benny. "There were too many of them."

Riddick glanced around, hands on hips. "They didn't take anyone else. They killed the cops that got in their way. Tried to kill Benny. Threatened to kill Harper." He paused to give the vampire on the floor a swift kick to the gut. "But they *took* Violet. If I had to guess, I'd say they needed her for something, which means she's still alive."

Nikolai sent a silent prayer up to whatever gods might be listening that Riddick was right. But at the same time, what would they need Violet for? What was happening to her? What did this have to do with her death threats and whoever trashed her home and shot at her?

"We need to call Seven," Harper said. "She was following up on a lead for me. If it panned out, I might have an idea who took Violet."

"Who?" Nikolai snarled, barely recognizing the cold, feral voice as his own.

Harper shook her head. "You're not going to like this."

Chapter Twenty-seven

Violet woke up tied to a chair. Again.

Jesus, wasn't once in a lifetime enough? *No*, not for Violet Marchand, apparently.

Ugh. And as if being tied to a chair with plastic zip ties—*again*—wasn't bad enough, her head felt like it might explode and her mouth tasted like she'd gargled with a dead rat. She recognized the symptoms of homemade roofies from the *last* time she'd been kidnapped.

But this kidnapping was different, she reminded herself. Nikolai wasn't watching over her this time.

Violet's eyes burned as she tried to stifle tears. There'd been so many bullets flying around the station. Was Nikolai still alive? Had they taken him, too?

Needing to know had her cracking one eye open a bit wider. Fluorescent light immediately assaulted her eyes and the pain almost made her throw up. It felt like someone was ramming an icepick through her eyeball into her brain.

But slowly, the pain dulled to merely agonizing, and she forced her eyes open again.

She was in what looked to be an old army barracks. Concrete walls and floor, metal-framed bunk beds shoved against the walls, fluorescent overhead lighting. No windows. Only one door.

About half a dozen men were in the room with her—vampires, if she hadn't missed her guess—all wearing black cargo pants and T-shirts, all armed with assault rifles and hunting knives.

And Nikolai was nowhere in sight. She was on her own.

The door opened and another man entered the room. Violet's stomach turned over. *Oh, Jesus, this can't be good.*

Miles looked utterly ridiculous in the mercenary chic the other men were effortlessly rocking. Instead, he looked like, well, an actuary playing dress-up.

He kneeled down beside her chair and held up a bottle of water, his eyes wide and hopeful like a puppy expecting a belly rub. Violet glanced at the water bottle and saw it was still sealed, so she nodded.

He twisted the top off the bottle and held it to her lips so she could drink. When she'd had enough, she turned her head away, and asked, "Miles, what the hell is going on? What have you done?"

Miles capped the water and set it on the ground beside him. "I did this for you, Violet. For us."

Inwardly she cringed at the adoration in his tone when he said her name. Obviously he was delusional about their past relationship. She was a psychiatrist, for God's sake. How the hell had she missed *that*?

"What do you mean, Miles?" she asked in her coolest chatting-with-a-deranged-maniac voice. "What did you do for me?"

"I became a vampire, of course."

With that startling revelation, he lifted his lips, showing off a brand-new set of razor-sharp, shiny white vampire fangs.

And as if that wasn't terrifying enough, he added, "And now I can make you one, too. We can be together *forever*, my dear. You'll finally be mine, just as you were meant to be."

"Oh, Jesus," she blurted as a wave of terror washed over her. "You really are nuts, aren't you? I'm not meant to be yours! I'll *never* be yours!"

His hand shot out with inhuman speed and slapped her across the face. Just a tap for a vampire, probably backed off to 10 percent strength or so. But to her poor human cheek, it felt like she'd done a face-plant onto a moving bullet train. She could feel her cheek swelling and taste blood on her tongue.

Then he was on his feet, grabbing a fistful of her hair and jerking her head back so that she was staring straight up into his face. "*I'm* nuts?" he snarled at her. "You're the one carrying on with a half-breed *murderer*! You're lucky I'm even still willing to have you!"

"All right now, Stats, that's about enough of that," a calm

voice intoned from behind them. "Why don't you take a break and let me have a little chat with the good doctor here?"

Miles continued to glare down at her, and she stubbornly maintained eye contact, as defiant as she could manage under the circumstances. It wasn't normally a good idea to provoke crazy people, but Violet understood that emotional people made mistakes. Mistakes created opportunities to escape. If she was to escape on her own, she needed to keep Miles emotional and off balance.

With one last snarl, Miles released her. She flinched as he kicked the water bottle across the room, and stalked off, slamming the door behind him as he left.

The sound of a throat clearing drew her attention to the man who'd just pulled up a metal folding chair in front of her own and straddled it backwards.

"I apologize for Miles's behavior. You know how new vamps are, don't you, doc? So moody and temperamental. All their emotions heightened to crazy levels." He shook his head. "But anyhow, we haven't been properly introduced," he said, his voice carrying a deceptively pleasant and non-threatening Southern accent. "I'm Marshall Briggs."

Violet narrowed her eyes on him. "Well, *Marshall Briggs*, I'd shake your hand, but mine seem to be *tied to this chair*."

He chuckled and shoved a hand through his dark blond hair.

"You're feisty. I like that."

Well, why don't you untie me and I'll show you how feisty I can be when I introduce my knee to your nuts?

"I'll assume you already know who I am since you kidnapped me," she intoned dryly. "And I'll also assume that I'm not here to impress you with my *feistiness*. So, what exactly is it that you want from me, Marshall Briggs?"

He leaned forward, offering her a pleasant smile that came nowhere close to reaching his glacial blue eyes. "Would you believe that I need you to help me make the world a better place?"

She shrugged a shoulder. "Sure. Why not? Why wouldn't I believe that a guy who had me kidnapped, tied to a chair, and beaten by my ex-boyfriend *wouldn't* want to make the world a better place? I mean, you're clearly a humanitarian."

"See, that's just the thing," he said, not bothering to acknowledge her sarcasm. "I'm kind of the *opposite* of a humanitarian. I'm a…vampiretarian? Is that a word? If it's not it should be."

The slap must have shaken her brain around a bit too much, because she was having a devil of a time keeping up with his train of thought. "You're fighting for vampire rights? Don't you guys already have those?"

His affable expression slipped. "We're merely tolerated by the humans. Despised by the shifters and *dhampyres*. We're ruled by a dictator and his little enforcer *whore* who won't even let us be who we are. And do you know who we are, doc? Who we're *supposed* to be?"

Oh, goodie, she thought. A zealot. The least reasonable people in the world were zealots. They never saw that anything they did was wrong. All sacrifices were deemed acceptable losses in the name of their beliefs. Of all the deranged psychopaths she'd seen in her career, none were as scary as zealots.

"I don't know," she answered carefully. "What do *you* think you're supposed to be?"

He smirked at her. "Spoken like a true shrink. We're predators, doc. A higher species. The top of the food chain. And yet our leader," he said, speaking the word *leader* with enough venom to make Violet shrink back in her chair a bit, "has us practically bowing down to humans and letting shifters and halfers *pretend* they're even worthy to breathe the same *air* as us vampires."

Violet didn't think it would do any good to point out that vampires didn't even need to breathe the same air as, well, *anyone* else, since they didn't breathe at all. So instead, she guessed, "You want to take over the council?"

He grinned at her like a proud papa whose little girl had just finished singing the ABC song for the first time. "Smart girl. Yes, we want to take over the council. And that's where *you* come in."

Oh, boy. "But I'm not on the council," she argued. "In case you haven't noticed, I'm not a vampire."

"You're not a vampire *yet*."

A chill skated down her spine. "If you turn me against my will, you'll go to jail."

"And *that* will be the first law we'll change when we take over the council. Under our rule, vampires will be able to change anyone they damn well please, just as it used to be back before humans knew we existed."

A zealot who longed for the good old days, when humans were nothing more than walking, talking Happy Meals. Awesome. If she was able to head shrink her way out of this one, it'd be a miracle.

"The head of the council is over 500 hundred years old," she told him as gently as she could manage. "He's the strongest vampire in the state—maybe even the world. The only vampire anywhere *close* to his strength is his wife." *You know, the one you called a whore?* She shook her head. "How can you possibly hope to overpower them to take control of the council?"

His answering smile was far too reasonable, considering how bat-shit crazy he was. "Well, of course we don't expect to do it *alone*."

And that's when the puzzle pieces all clicked into place. The guerilla warfare garb. The abandoned military bunker. "You're building an army," she whispered, horrified.

And he wanted to recruit her patients. Because even though Briggs could make as many vamps as he wanted, older vampires were stronger, faster. Even with their various psychological issues, her patients would make better soldiers than any newly turned vampires.

He pointed his fingers like a gun at her and winked. "Again, smart girl. I knew there must be a reason why Miles was so crazy for you. You know, other than the obvious."

Well, the *crazy* part was certainly right. "What does Miles have to do with this?" she asked.

"Honestly?" Briggs looked behind him to make sure no one was listening before saying, "Miles approached one of my guys about being turned. He was apparently sick of getting passed over for promotions and such at work by vampire candidates. He thought it was a form of affirmative action. We were going to turn the dude down. Frankly, he's an annoying little fuck. But then he mentioned his girlfriend, the lovely Dr. Violet Marchand, therapist to—allegedly—every vampire, shifter, psychic, and halfer in town. Smart move not keeping your client list in your home or office, by the way. Although, it would've made things much easier for you if you'd been just a *smidge* less concerned with your patients' privacy."

Violet would've rubbed her aching temples if her hands weren't tied. They'd been in her home and office looking for her client list. They wanted her to help convince her patients and ex patients to turn on the council and join their army. She couldn't even express how crazy that idea was, so instead, she asked, "If you need my help, why did you try to kill me outside the bar?"

He looked confused for a moment, then his expression cleared and he said, "Oh, that wasn't us. It was Miles. I'd say he was a little irked to see his girlfriend making out with a *dhampyre*. Trust me when I say that if *I'd* wanted you dead, you'd *be* dead."

She chose to ignore the last part of that statement. "I'm not his girlfriend."

He smirked at her. "I'm getting that. I'm starting to see why the death threats didn't send you running into his arms for love, support, and protection like we'd hoped, either." He shrugged. "Oh, well. Snagging you from the police station worked just as well, I suppose. It just took us some time to build up the numbers we needed to get it done. Guess we should have just gone with the simplest plan to begin with, huh?"

She blinked at him. The death threats hadn't been real at all. They'd just wanted her to run to Miles so that he could protect her and convince her to help them with…whatever their plan was. "So, what was Miles supposed to do if I had gone to him for protection?"

"Bring you to me. Let me convince you that the council had no interest in keeping you safe, but that I—that *we*—could."

She eyed him skeptically, and he laughed, adding, "Well, there are *some* people who find me charming and convincing, doc. Believe it or not."

"And what happens to my non-vampire patients?" she asked. "The shifters and halfers?" The *dhampyres*. Nikolai. "What do you intend to do with them?"

His answering smile was a blood-chilling mix of maniacal and friendly. "They're abominations, doc. The world will be a better place without them."

She knew by the fanatical gleam in his eye that her choices were simple: help with their plan, or die. But if he was right, and the shifters, halfers, and *dhampyres* were abominations and Briggs and Miles were the superior species…well, that wasn't a world Violet wanted any part of.

Holding her head high and doing everything in her power to keep her voice from quivering, Violet looked Briggs in the eye and said, "I won't help you. And you should know that my friends—the abominations you want to destroy—will come for me."

"Oh, we'll see," he said. "I think you'll change your mind."

Briggs turned and pulled a syringe full of liquid from his tactical vest. Violet did her best to maintain composure, not wanting to give this bastard the satisfaction of knowing she was terrified, but she trembled regardless. What the hell was in that syringe? What was it going to do to her? Knock her out again?

He leaned over and causally injected it into her arm without bothering to wipe her skin down with disinfectant. Great. Even if she lived through this she'd most likely end up with a raging infection.

But that and every other thought in her head fled as heat seemed to course through her veins and the room around her started to spin. "What the hell did you give me?"

Was it her imagination, or was she slurring her words? Was her tongue thicker all of a sudden? And why was her head suddenly so damn heavy?

Briggs leaned down and shined a penlight into each of her eyes. "Oh, don't worry about it, doc," he said, his voice rife with mock compassion. "It's just a little something to loosen your tongue and make you feel more agreeable to disclosing your full client list."

"Never," she slurred.

He stroked his hand over her hair gently. "We'll see, doc. We'll see."

Chapter Twenty-eight

Nikolai couldn't sit still. Furious anxiety rippled through him, making his hands shake as he paced the length of Harper's conference room.

Riddick watched him from the corner, and Benny and Harper had their heads bent together in a whispered conversation. On the other side of the room, shackled to the conference room table, sat the vampire who'd gotten a taste of Harper's wrath.

Nikolai wanted to put a gun to the bastard's head or beat the shit out of him to encourage him to divulge where Miles was holding Violet, but Harper had given Riddick strict instructions to shoot Nikolai in the leg if he tried. And the longer the bastard sat there, smirking, refusing to tell them anything, Nikolai was starting to think it'd be worth taking a bullet just to hear the smug bastard scream as he ripped him limb from limb.

"Tell me again why we're not just torturing Violet's location out of him," Nikolai said.

Harper sighed. "Because it won't work. I'm psychic, remember? The only vision I got off him told me he's a vampire right's zealous nut bag, and zealots are willing to be tortured. This one's been trained to handle it and not spill. I have another plan."

Nikolai scrubbed a hand over his face. "What plan? We're just sitting here doing nothing while Violet's out there…"

He trailed off, not even wanting to think the rest of that sentence. Anything could be happening to her. Could've already happened to her.

Nikolai slammed his fists down onto the table. "Goddammit!"

Their prisoner let out a raspy chuckle. "Someone's a little high-strung, huh?"

Nikolai snarled at him, but Harper merely shook her head before saying, "Wow, you've got a death wish, huh, bro?"

The vampire sneered at her. "There's nothing you can do to get me to talk, whore."

Riddick's chair squeaked as he leaned forward and cracked his knuckles. "Unless you want to find out what it's like to have your own severed arm shoved up your ass, you'll watch what you say to my wife."

The vampire seemed to consider the threat and must have found it a credible one, because he sniffed and grumbled, "I won't tell you anything. No matter what you do to me."

Harper raised a brow at him. "What makes you think *I'm* going to do anything to you?" She snorted. "Please. You aren't worth my effort."

This seemed to confuse the vampire as much as it confused

Nikolai. "Then why the fuck am I here?"

"You're here for me."

All eyes in the room immediately went to the doorway, and what—or rather, *who*—he saw there suddenly made Nikolai feel a whole lot better about their chances of getting the vampire to talk.

Hunter, head of the vampire council, strode into the room, looking slightly put out at having been summoned to Harper's office at this time of night.

An uneasy chill skated down Nikolai's spine, just as it always did when he was in Hunter's presence.

In Nikolai's time with Sentry, he'd killed all manner of paranormal creatures. Young, old, weak, strong, vampire, shifter…it didn't matter. Nikolai had experience killing it. But Hunter? He was something altogether different than anything or anyone Nikolai had ever known.

Hunter predated all written records of vampires in North America, having been born sometime around 1492. Sure, there were stories of vampires older than that in Europe, but they were just that: stories. There was no evidence that any of them were still roaming the earth.

So, as far as anyone knew, Hunter was the oldest vampire in existence. And the power that came from being the oldest…well, it practically oozed out of his pores.

That kind of power made Nikolai edgy. Made him realize there were things in the world that were actually a danger to him, no matter how many kills he had under his belt. Made him feel almost human.

It was disconcerting. Kind of nice and terrifying all at the same time.

Hunter sat down next to Harper with a deep sigh and asked, "Why am I here instead of at home in bed with my wife?"

Harper jerked her thumb in the other vampire's direction. "This asshat's friends kidnapped Violet and he won't tell us where they are or why they did it."

Hunter glanced over at the vampire, who shrank in his seat, eyes widened in terror. "So it's *your* fault I'm not at home in bed with my wife?"

His tone was bland, but the look he was giving the vampire was sharp enough to separate flesh from bone, and if this asshole wasn't somehow involved with whoever had taken Violet, he'd feel sorry for him. But as it stood, Nikolai found he couldn't care less.

"He called me a whore, too," Harper added helpfully.

Hunter's eyes narrowed and Nikolai thought he heard the other vampire whimper a little bit. "That's no way to speak to a lady. A hundred-year-old vampire should know better and have better manners than that," he chided.

The vampire—who looked incredibly pale, even for an undead creature—shifted uncomfortably in his chair and said, "I-I c-can't tell you a-anything. I s-swear."

Harper turned to Nikolai. "OK, grab some pliers. We'll go ahead and try this your way."

"Don't waste time on the fingernails. Go straight for the balls," Riddick suggested. "Never fails."

Nikolai shot the vampire what he was sure was a feral grin before Hunter held up a hand and said, "Not yet. I don't think he's *refusing* to tell us, I believe he's been compelled *not* to tell us by an older vampire. Isn't that right, child?"

The vampire was sweating blood at this point and couldn't seem to choke out any words, but he did manage to nod.

Harper sighed. "Well, shit. Do you think you can break the compulsion to get the info we need, Hunter?"

Hunter raised a brow at her, looking decidedly insulted.

She threw her hands up in surrender. "Sorry, your worship. Didn't mean to insult your…vampirehood."

Hunter shook his head. "I've asked you repeatedly not to call me that."

She cocked her head to one side and studied him before asking, "Do you prefer your eminence? Your highness? Khal

Hunter?"

"Grand poobah?" Benny suggested.

Hunter let out another world-weary sigh. "I suppose 'your worship' will do after all."

Nikolai swallowed a growl of frustration and impatience. "Can we please—for the love of God—just get the information we need from this *mudak* so I can go get Violet?"

Hunter turned a terrifying smile on the vampire who was now openly weeping. "This might hurt a bit."

Chapter Twenty-nine

"I don't understand why she called me a boy."

Riddick sighed. "Harper didn't call you a boy, Seven. She was quoting a movie line."

"'Bye bye, boys—have fun storming the castle' is what Miracle Max and his wife said before Westley, Inigo, and Fezzik went to rescue Buttercup at the end of *The Princess Bride*," Hunter added.

Seven still looked confused. "We're not storming a castle. It's clearly some kind of old abandoned military bunker."

Lucas looped an arm around his wife's shoulders. "It's Harper. Life'll be a lot easier for you if you just assume everything she says will be confusing on some level."

Nikolai could barely pay attention to the group's banter as he watched dozens of armed guards—armed *vampire* guards—walking the perimeter of the old compound. Their view from the ridge where they'd parked Hunter's SUV was clear, giving them an unobstructed view of exactly what they were up against.

He'd been up against worse for less, he decided. They were outnumbered 20—no, more like 30—to one, but with Violet inside? He knew he'd gladly take on twice that many by himself to get her back safely.

"I don't like the odds," Seven said.

"You don't have to go in with us if you're scared, sweetheart," Riddick answered in a tender voice he apparently reserved for his wife, daughter, and sister.

Seven blinked at him. "I'm not scared. I just meant it's not a fair fight. The five of us can cut through these baby vampires without really trying."

It was true. The vampires guarding the facility seemed to be newly turned. None of them would fare well against the oldest vampire in existence, three *dhampyres*, and a werewolf. But given their sheer numbers and weapons, the threat the vampires posed couldn't be taken too lightly. To say nothing of the fact that Violet could get caught in the crossfire if things went south.

"Their weapons go a good ways toward evening the odds," Nikolai murmured.

"Seven and I can take care of that," Hunter said. "We'd just need a distraction. Something that gets all of them to draw their weapons at once."

Riddick snorted. "Too bad we left Harper at home. No one can cause a distraction like her."

"True," Hunter said. "But it's best that she's not here. She's a good fighter, but we already have one human to worry about tonight. It's better for our concentration if we don't have to worry about her safety."

"You know she's not likely to forget you having Mischa barricade her and Benny in the house, right?" Riddick asked.

"I'm aware," Hunter said dryly. "I fully expect to find myself with a home covered in toilet paper and inexplicable subscriptions to every gay porn site she can find."

"That's if you're lucky," Seven mumbled.

"Can you tell how many vampires are inside with Violet?" Nikolai asked Hunter.

"I can sense six minds in the room. One human—Violet, I presume—and five vampires."

"And you think you can disarm those five, plus the ones out here if you have a distraction of some kind?"

"With Seven's help, yes."

"And can you tell where Violet is in the room? Is she far away from the door?"

"She's in the back of the building, a good distance from the door."

Riddick narrowed his eyes on Nikolai. "Whatever you're thinking, I don't like it. You need to keep your head in the game, man. Keep it together."

Riddick was right. Nikolai knew he was distracted—his worry

over Violet's safety scattering his thoughts all over the place. He wasn't normally like this on a mission. He was usually calm and collected.

But then again, usually the woman he loved wasn't directly in the line of fire.

Panic flickered through him at the thought of losing her, but he didn't let the thought take hold. Not here. Not now. Instead, he shoved it to the back of his mind as he looked back toward the compound.

"I have an idea about how to create the distraction you need to disarm the guards," Nikolai said. "But I have one question for you first, Hunter."

The ancient vampire frowned at him. "What is it?"

"How attached are you to your car?"

Chapter Thirty

Gunshots rang out in the distance, but Violet could scarcely lift her head to see what was going on. Whatever drug Briggs had given her left her feeling foggy-headed and weak. But even her drug-soaked, addled brain realized what the sounds of destruction, panic, and chaos in the distance meant.

Nikolai was here.

He was *alive* and he'd come for her!

"I told you he'd come," Violet said, trying to ignore the drunken-sounding slur of her words.

"Yeah, yeah," Briggs muttered. "You told me so. Guess that makes you feel all intellectually superior, huh? Well, it just means we're going to have to speed up our timetable. I need you to give me those names now, doc. Patients, former patients, random vamps you've passed on the street…I want them all."

Her brain felt like it was being torn in half. Part of her demanded that she give him whatever he wanted. She'd like to think that was the drug doing whatever it was supposed to do to her.

The other part of her, the rational, logical part that knew Nikolai was just outside and was coming in after her? Well, that part wanted to tell Briggs to take his demands and shove them straight up his ass.

What the hell was she supposed to do? Violet forced herself to take a deep, calming breath. She wished Harper was here. Harper would know what to do. She was always tough, cool, and in control. What would Harper do right now?

Violet lifted her head and looked at Briggs through dry, gritty, bleary eyes. The bastard looked so smug sitting there, leaning forward in his chair, waiting for her to spill her guts, so sure she had no choice but to comply. It was in that moment, looking into his smug, irritatingly calm face that she knew exactly what Harper would do.

Violet head-butted the bastard.

He grunted as his head snapped back, then he leaned forward to spit a mouthful of blood at her feet. "Gotta say, I'm surprised, doc. Didn't think you had that in you."

Neither had she, really. But it felt surprisingly good. Other than the blinding headache that came with head-butting someone. Harper hadn't warned her about that. *Ouch.*

"I'm not telling you *anything*," she said through gritted teeth.

She couldn't hold back a gasp when he snagged a fistful of her hair and forced her head back. The pure hatred in his eyes as he stared down at her sent a shiver of pure dread down her spine.

"You know, I promised Miles he could have you when I got what I needed from you. But there's one thing Miles forgot about. The first lesson in how vampires think and act."

She wasn't at all sure she wanted to know, but Violet, for some reason, still asked, "What's that?"

"Vampires lie."

"Get ready!" Nikolai yelled as he jumped behind the wheel.

"Don't kill anyone!" Hunter yelled back. "Snap as many necks as you want, but no severed heads. Understood?"

Riddick and Lucas grumbled, but Nikolai and Seven nodded. He imagined Seven was being truthful in her agreement. Nikolai wasn't entirely sure he was, though. If Violet was hurt—or worse—he couldn't promise he wouldn't kill every vampire in his path.

He sped down the uneven ground of the ravine toward the bunker, dodging trees and bushes as best he could, going airborne at times. Good thing Hunter had said he didn't give a shit about the car, because it would surely never be the same after this.

The vampires raised their weapons as the car broke through the last of the brush and skidded into the open ground around the bunker. One even managed to squeeze off a shot that splintered the windshield into a spider web of cracks. Nikolai kept going.

In the rearview mirror, he saw Seven raise her hands, and with that one motion, the vampires' guns were yanked from their grasps and held aloft, high above the tallest tree branches in the woods around them. Next to her, Hunter did the same, and the guns exploded in midair, raining gunpowder and metal shavings down onto the heads of the vampires.

He'd take a moment when this was all over and Violet was safe to appreciate how utterly—what would Harper say?—*badass* telekinesis was. But at the moment, he still had work to do.

Now that he was certain he wasn't going to get shot, Nikolai yanked the emergency brake and skidded into a spin, letting the car slam into the bunker's metal door. He kicked what was left of the windshield out and leapt onto the hood of the car, ready to face the now-unarmed vampires who rushed him all at once.

What came next could only be called an explosion of violence.

Lucas burst through the clearing in full wolf form, snagging the first vampire he encountered in his massive jaws. The wolf shook his head with enough force to snap the vampire's neck. When the vampire went limp in his grasp, the wolf dropped him and moved on to his next target.

Seven caught a vampire who started to go after the wolf in the back of the head with her elbow, and when he pitched forward, she spun around with inhuman speed, got in front of him, and drove her knee up into his face. The vampire spit a mouthful of teeth onto the ground before passing out as Seven glanced back to check on her husband, who huffed out a noise that Nikolai took to be a wolf's version of "thank you."

Nikolai jumped up and off the car to avoid the snapping jaws of two vampires who lunged at him. On his way down, he drove his elbow into the back of one vampire's head, and caught the other on the chin with a kick that sent him reeling backward, unconscious.

Next to him, Riddick seemed to be tearing through a throng of advancing vampires and, God help him, he looked like he was having fun. Elbows and blood and teeth were flying everywhere and the crazy bastard looked to be…smiling.

Hunter didn't even have to wade into the violence to do his part. He strolled casually toward the bunker, flinging vampires out of his path and into the woods with nothing more than casual flicks of his wrists.

"Go get her! We got this!" Riddick yelled over the melee as he tossed the body of a limp vampire at another who was rushing him.

Nikolai gave Riddick a terse nod of thanks, and with one swift kick, the bunker's already battered metal door snapped off its hinges. He avoided seeking Violet out. Instead, he focused on the vampires—one, two, three, four—who rushed him.

Blood sprayed the walls, bones cracked, and the odor of fear and sweat permeated the room, but the vampires didn't stand a chance. Nikolai took out every vamp that came at him with ruthless efficiency.

That's when he saw Violet. Bloodied, head down, tied to an old office chair. Blood pooled at her feet.

He nearly doubled over, fighting the urge to vomit. Oh, Jesus…was she dead?

He wouldn't survive losing her.

No one here would survive if he lost her.

She shivered and the sense of relief that took hold in him nearly buckled his knees. She was alive! Moving faster than he'd ever moved in his life, he raced across the room toward Violet. His only purpose, the only thing he had to do in this life, was getting her to safety.

Then it occurred to him that there'd been five hostiles in the building with Violet. He'd only taken out four.

A tall, blond vampire stepped out from behind a concrete pillar and squatted behind Violet, using her body as a shield. And as if that wasn't bad enough, he pressed a six-inch hunting knife with a serrated blade against the delicate skin of her throat.

Don't kill them, Hunter had said.

All bets were off with this one. This one was dying. Soon.

"Stop right there," the man said.

Nikolai stopped, his boots skidding across the blood-soaked concrete. The monster that lived inside him, the one he was barely keeping hold of at the moment, howled in frustration.

He stared at the vampire, doing some quick calculations in his head. Nikolai knew he was faster than the vampire, but was he fast enough to take him down before he could cut Violet? He wasn't sure. He couldn't take the chance.

"What do you want?" Nikolai asked.

Violet's head lifted and her eyes fluttered open at the sound of his voice, but Nikolai refused to acknowledge it. She was alive. He was going to get her out of this. That was all that mattered.

The vampire smiled. "Well, now, you seem much more agreeable than the good doc, here."

Nikolai spread his arms wide. "I'll give you whatever you want. Just let her go."

He shook his head. "But see, that's just the thing. I don't *need* anything from you. I need answers from *her*. I need to know where she keeps her patient records, and let's just say she's been less than cooperative. So, I'm afraid I'll be taking her with me. And you're going to need to let me go."

Over my dead body.

"You don't need her for that," Nikolai said as calmly as he

could manage. "I had her under surveillance for months. I can give you the names and locations of every one of her patients."

"No." The word came out as a whisper, but Violet's eyes blazed and screamed at him.

He met her eyes and held them, forcing everything he felt for her into that one gaze. "I need you to trust me, *kotehok*. Can you do that?"

She blinked at him slowly as he tried to pretend her answer didn't mean everything to him.

Nikolai knew his request wasn't easy for her. He'd betrayed her trust before, and her patients meant so much to her. She'd never let anyone hurt them. Hell, she'd endured torture just to protect them. And now he was asking her to trust him after he'd just offered her patients to a madman on a silver platter.

But after a tense moment where Nikolai was pretty sure his heart had taken up permanent residence in his throat, she nodded. And if he wasn't mistaken, he thought he saw one corner of her mouth quirk up a tiny bit.

That tiny little smile told him everything he needed to know. Not only did she trust him, but she had every confidence in him, knowing he'd get them both out of this. Her trust was the greatest gift he ever could have received.

The moment was ruined when the vampire chuckled. "Aw,

this is so sweet. It's like watching a Lifetime channel movie play out in real time. But seriously, pal, I'll need you to call off your scary-looking friend back there." He pressed the knife blade into Violet's skin just enough to elicit a tiny gasp and a pin-prick of blood from her. "I mean, sure, I need her, but that doesn't mean I won't hurt her."

Nikolai didn't need to turn around to know who was behind him. "Riddick, get out. I've got this."

Riddick took a step forward so that Nikolai could see him out of the corner of his eye. "No way, man. This guy's gonna—"

"Go!" Nikolai shouted.

"I'm not leaving without Violet," Riddick said.

Nikolai raised a brow at the vamp. "She can go, right? You don't need her since you have me, yes?"

The vampire rubbed at the scruff on his chin with his free hand and grinned. "Sure thing, pal. She was kind of a pill, anyway."

Then he shoved Violet in her wheeled office chair to Riddick, who grabbed her, chair and all, and picked her up like she was no heavier than a child. Nikolai let out his first easy breath since Violet was taken when Riddick ran for the door.

The vampire took advantage of Nikolai's distraction by grabbing him around the throat with one arm and pressing the blade to his carotid artery. Nikolai swallowed his rage, forcing himself to feel nothing. Violet was safe with Riddick. That was all that mattered.

"Didn't imagine there was any way you'd *really* go quietly," the vampire hissed in his ear.

Unfortunately, Violet chose that moment to look back at him over Riddick's shoulder. When she saw the knife pressed to his throat, she let out a shriek that Nikolai knew he'd never in his life forget.

Don't watch, kotehok. *Turn away.*

Violet pleaded with Riddick to put her down, to help Nikolai, begged him to stop, but Riddick—thank God—didn't listen to her pleas. It wasn't long before they were safely out of the building.

Time to let the monster slip its leash.

With one elbow strike, Nikolai created enough room between his body and the vampire's to draw his own knife. The vampire roared in frustration and swung. Metal clashed.

The vampire didn't have a prayer of winning this fight. Nikolai was faster, stronger, better trained, and most importantly, he had pure, unadulterated *rage* on his side. For every slice the vampire inflicted, Nikolai scored two.

And each one felt better than the last.

He didn't let up, either. Didn't give his opponent time to

relax or rest. Nikolai continued to push forward, forcing the vampire to stay on the defensive.

The vamp swung his knife desperately in an arch at Nikolai's face, but the blow was weak, sloppy. Nikolai easily dodged the blade, then kicked the vampire's hand. The knife went flying.

Nikolai dropped, spun, and neatly swept the vampire's legs out from under him. He went down on his back hard, arms flailing. In a matter of seconds, Nikolai had him pinned on the bloody concrete floor, with his hands around the vampire's throat as he slowly started squeezing.

"Any last words?" Nikolai snarled.

"Fuck…you," the vampire choked out.

"Pathetic waste of last words, *mudak*."

Nikolai tightened his grip until he felt the vampire's esophagus crumble beneath his fingertips. The monster demanded he grab a fistful of the guy's hair and slam his head down into the concrete, which Nikolai did with barely restrained glee.

He grabbed his knife and held it to the vampire's throat, steadying the blade so that it would take only a few slices to sever the bastard's head.

"Stop! I said don't kill anyone! What part of that wasn't clear?" Hunter said, clearly exasperated.

"Oh, come on, man," Riddick said, "at least let him kill *this* one. That's the one who hurt Violet! She said his name is Briggs. He's leading some kind of rebellion against you and the council. He deserves what he gets!"

"All the more reason why I need *this* one alive. We need to determine if this is an isolated group, or if there are more of them out there."

Nikolai's hands started shaking with the need to slit this vampire's throat. To destroy the one who'd dared to lay his hands on Violet. To make sure she was well and truly safe, once and for all.

"Put it down or I'll take it from you," Hunter warned.

He could do it, too. Without ever laying a hand on him. But how fast could Hunter knock the knife out of his hand? Faster than Nikolai could sever the layers of skin and muscle and bone that held the vampire's head on his shoulders? Maybe not…

"Nikolai," Violet whispered. "Please."

Nikolai's head shot up. Riddick had carried Violet in with him. Bringing her back in here had been stupid on Riddick's part, but at least he'd gotten her out of that damn chair.

Her hand lulled limply against Riddick's shoulder, but her blue eyes were locked on Nikolai and bright with tears and a mix of fear and…something he couldn't quite identify. Was she afraid of him?

That's when it occurred to him that she'd just seen him joyfully beat a man (a vicious, sadistic vampire, but still…) to unconsciousness and prepare to take his head off.

She'd seen the monster.

Fury threatened to overtake him. God dammit! He'd never wanted her to see that side of him. Never wanted her to know—to see—what he was truly capable of.

He dropped the knife, slowly stood up, and crossed the room, holding her gaze as he moved. She was so tired. He could practically see her strength draining by the second. It looked like she was clinging to consciousness by nothing but sheer force of will.

"Violet, I—"

The sharp bark of a Glock split the night air. Pain seared Nikolai's chest. Violet screamed as blood bloomed all over the front of his shirt.

Nikolai dropped to his knees as chaos once again erupted around him.

Miles rushed into the building from where he'd apparently been hiding in the woods. He must have run before Hunter destroyed the other vamps' guns. Pathetic little coward.

"If I'm going to Midvale," Miles shouted, "at least I know she won't end up with you!"

Riddick set Violet down and she immediately crawled to Nikolai's side, tears streaming down her cheeks. Hunter waved a hand at Miles and the gun flew from his grip, but not before he managed to fire off one last shot that hit Nikolai in the shoulder.

He fell back at the impact. The last thing he heard before the darkness claimed him was Violet screaming and begging him not to die.

Chapter Thirty-one

It'd been two days, three hours, 42 minutes and—Violet glanced down at her watch—20 seconds since the surgeons had removed two bullets from Nikolai's body. One had pierced his lung, which was one of the few wounds severe enough to actually endanger a *dhampyre*. Only a bullet through the heart or brain would've dropped him faster.

But he was healing now, and everyone assured her he'd recover, but seeing him like this, pale and weak in a hospital bed, was almost more than Violet could stand.

She held his hand to her cheek, silently willing him to hurry up, heal, and come back to her. Until he opened those beautiful green eyes of his and smirked up at her, she wasn't going to be able to take a full breath.

The door to Nikolai's room swung open and Harper strolled in.

She jerked her chin in Nikolai's direction. "How's the patient today?"

"Better," Violet said, because maybe if she said it enough, it'd be true one of these times.

Harper hoisted herself up so that she could sit on the little nightstand next to Nikolai's bed. She shoved an untouched lunch tray out of her way. "I have some good news. Oh, hey, look! Green Jello!

I love this stuff."

Violet watched as Harper peeled back the cover on her prize and dug in with childlike glee. It quickly became apparent that Harper had lost her train of thought and needed a nudge back in the right direction. "What's the news, Harper?"

"Well, it would seem that the little vampire uprising has been officially thwarted. Briggs and his group were the only ones involved. No out-of-towners. And since our guys pretty much stomped the crap out of Briggs's guys—yay us!—it's all over."

That was good news. Violet was sure she'd care more about it once Nikolai was awake. "What's going to happen to them?"

Harper grinned manically. "That's the best part. Hunter left their punishment up to Mischa."

Violet winced. Wow. They'd be begging for death by the time Mischa was done with them. Normally, she had sympathy for condemned prisoners. But this time? Violet couldn't bring herself to care too much what happened to Briggs, Miles, and all the other clueless losers who sought to take control from the most stable leader the vampires had ever had. They deserved what they got. "What about the human cops?"

"The legal weasel took care of them. Nikolai's no longer a suspect in any of their cases. He's totally clear. The best part, though? Cunningham got busted back to beat cop for what he did to

Nikolai."

Violet allowed herself a small smile at the thought of Cunningham in a years-old, too-tight blue uniform, walking a beat, writing out parking tickets.

"You look like hammered dog shit," Harper said around a mouthful of Jello.

Violet imagined that was a polite description of how she looked. She'd gone way too long without a shower, and her clothes were so wrinkled and blood-covered they looked like she'd pulled them out of a dumpster. "Gee, thanks. You look pretty, too."

As usual, Harper ignored her sarcasm. "Have you slept at all? Eaten anything?"

How could she possibly sleep and eat while Nikolai was in this bed, recovering from major surgery after being *shot*? Shot because of *her*?

Harper dropped her empty Jello cup and let out a disgusted groan. "Look, I can see the self-loathing all over your face. Cut that shit out, OK? None of this is your fault. He would've done anything to get you out of there safely. The National Guard and a whole horde of Dothraki couldn't have stopped him. So, the last thing he needs is for you to sit here, feeling sorry for yourself, getting weak and sick because you're too lame to take care of yourself. It's a douchebag move and I'm not going to let you do it. He deserves better."

Violet blinked up at her, stunned. "You really suck at offering sympathy, you know that?"

Harper made another rude noise. "Suck it up, Buttercup. You're fine, he's going to be fine. The bad guys are probably being basted in pickle juice and staked to fire ant colonies as we speak." She waved her arms around and added, "I'm declaring this room a no-brooding zone. You need to get out of here, take a shower—seriously, you stink, Vi—and get something to eat. I'll stay with him until you get back."

Violet frowned. "I think—"

Harper grabbed her arm, lifted her out of her chair, and gave her a gentle shove toward the door. "I don't want you to think right now. Just be pretty instead, OK?"

Everything Harper had said was so insulting on so many levels that Violet was momentarily stunned speechless. But the worst part? The part that chafed like a cheap, polyester pair of panties?

She knew Harper was right.

If he was awake, Nikolai would insist she take care of herself before worrying about him. He'd be pissed if she let herself get sick in order to maintain some kind of bedside vigil for him.

Besides, she needed a little time to figure out exactly what she wanted to say to Nikolai when he woke up. She figured she should probably go easy on him rather than blurting out, *I love you and want to have your babies* at him the second he opened his eyes.

And it wasn't like anyone had ever won an argument with Harper Hall, anyway. What choice did she really have in all this?

Violet heaved a huge sigh. "You promise you'll stay with him? I don't want him to wake up alone."

Harper waved her off. "Yes, yes. Now get out. We'll be fine. Pretty sure I saw a Shasta and a pudding cup over here somewhere…"

Chapter Thirty-two

The first thing Nikolai became aware of as he drifted back to the land of the living was the combined smell of antiseptic and hospital-grade laundry detergent. It wasn't a pleasant combination.

And what the hell had died in his mouth? It tasted like he'd been sucking on day-old roadkill.

Memories of the fight at the bunker flooded back to him. The vampires, the smell of gunpowder in the air as Hunter destroyed their weapons…

The look in Violet's eyes as she watched him nearly slice a vampire's head off.

"Violet!"

He forced his eyes open and struggled to sit up, momentarily shocked at how much pain that simple motion caused. Jesus. How could two little bullets cause so much pain?

Small hands shoved him back down into the bed, eliciting another pained grunt from his raw throat. "Whoa, there, fireball. Just cool your jets. Your girl is fine. But you're not going anywhere just yet."

Nikolai looked up from his position flat on his back and found a grinning Harper Hall standing over him. "Welcome back, Comrade. I was starting to wonder if you were going to die on us after all."

"What the hell happened?" he ground out. "Where's Violet? What's going on?"

Harper quickly filled in the blanks of his memory, and let him know what had happened while he was unconscious. He took his first relieved breath—which still hurt quite a bit, damn it—since he woke up. Violet was safe. But why wasn't she here?

He groaned. "I fucked up. She saw me at my worst. Is that why she left?"

Harper rolled her eyes. "Oh, Jesus, you're as bad as she is. All brooding and self-loathing and *oh, no one can ever love me because I'm such a fuck-up.*" She blew a raspberry at him. "It's bullshit. You wanna know why she's not here? Because I made her leave. I kicked her out because she hadn't eaten, hadn't slept, hadn't showered, hadn't done anything other than sit there, holding your hand, waiting for your sorry ass to wake up."

Come back to me.

He thought he'd been dreaming, or hallucinating, courtesy of all the pain meds they'd obviously been pumping him full of. But if what Harper said was true, then that *had* been Violet's voice he heard, luring him back to consciousness.

He struggled to sit up again, and couldn't even gasp as the pain stole his breath. "I need to go to her," he wheezed.

"That's lovely," Harper said dryly, "but I don't think you're ready just yet. One of those bullets pierced your lung. Even for a dude with your super healing powers, that'll take some recovery time. How about I call her for you?"

No way. They'd already wasted too much time. He wasn't going to sit here and waste any more of it. "I'm going. With or without your help."

Harper crossed her arms over her chest. "Why? So you can do the oh-I'm-such-a-bad-guy-for-you-and-you- deserve-better dance some more? 'Cause I'm pretty sure that shit can wait until she gets back."

"No," he said through gritted teeth. "I know she deserves better, but I don't care anymore. I love her. I don't want to spend another minute of my life without her."

Harper's answering smile was bright as the sun. "Well, in that case, what are we waiting for? Let's get out of here."

Thank God. "Great. But I have a couple of stops to make first."

Chapter Thirty-three

Violet grabbed a hair tie and wound her still-wet hair into a sloppy ponytail as she raced for the door. She couldn't believe she'd slept that long! She'd only intended to be gone from the hospital for an hour or two, not six!

And why the hell wasn't Harper answering her phone? What if something had happened? What if Nikolai had taken a turn for the worse? What if—

She yanked her front door open and stopped short at the sight that greeted her.

Nikolai stood in her doorway, arms braced on the frame, as if he'd been working up the energy to knock. He looked pale and shaky, and seemed to be favoring his left side.

Joy at seeing him awake and right in front of her warred with her concern for his health. Surely the doctors hadn't released him this soon.

"Why are you here? Are you okay?" she asked.

"Not really. My lungs are on fire and my ribs hurt like a bitch." He paused and reached out to ease a strand of wet hair behind her ear. "But seeing you makes it so that I can finally breathe again."

She smiled, her eyes filling with tears—the good kind for

once. "I was on my way back to the hospital. Why did you leave?"

"Because we needed to talk, and I didn't want to wait another minute."

Her smiled faltered. In her vast experience, nothing good was ever prefaced with those four words. "Okay. Do you need to sit down?"

"Yes, but the only way to get my audience to stay in the car is to be out in the open where they can see me."

That's when she noticed Nikolai's SUV parked in front of her building. Harper and Benny were hanging out the windows, watching their every move, and Seven and Lucas were seated cross-legged on the hood, also focused on their exchange. Even little Haven had her head craned in their direction from her position in her car seat. Riddick was the only one who wasn't shamelessly eavesdropping from his position in the back seat next to his daughter.

"You brought…everyone," she said, awed.

He grimaced. "Not intentionally. Harper kind of insisted." He waved a hand in their direction. "Just ignore them. First of all, I need to apologize to you. It was my duty to protect you, and I failed."

Violet's throat tightened up. "You rescued me. I'm safe. You don't owe me anything anymore."

He raked a hand through his hair and blew out a harsh

breath. "I'm saying this wrong. I meant, yes, it was my duty to protect you, but it was never really about duty. From the beginning, all I ever really wanted was to be with you. I'm yours. And I'm here to convince you to be mine."

She choked out a laugh. "*Convince* me? You think you have to *convince* me?"

He blinked at her. "Well…yes?"

Harper waved her hands at them and yelled, "Hey! Exhibit A is getting antsy in here. Can I bring her out?"

Nikolai let out an exasperated growl. "Yes, yes, fine."

"Exhibit A?" Violet asked.

Harper hauled a huge box up to the door and set it at Nikolai's feet. "Yep. Exhibit A in the case of Nikolai loves Violet." She winked at her. "It's a doozy."

"Fine, thank you, now go away," Nikolai hissed.

Harper frowned at him. "Okay, Mr. Grouchy Pants. You're *welcome*."

And with that, she tossed her hair over her shoulder and went back to the SUV.

Violet glanced down at the box. "You brought presents?"

"Yes. This one is to prove that I want to build a life with you.

I want all the same things you want. Anything you need, I want to give it to you. Normal things that other human men can give you—I'm capable of those things, too. I love you, Violet. More than anything or anyone. More than my own life."

Her eyes misted over again. That was maybe the most beautiful thing anyone had ever said to her. She glanced down at the box.

His eyes were warm as he smiled at her. "Open it."

Violet peeled back the box flaps and gasped as a little dog popped up like it had been spring-loaded and started licking her nose. "Oh, my God," she squealed. "You got me a dog!"

"I got *us* a dog. From the shelter. I thought if I made the decision of which one to adopt, it would save you from feeling bad about the ones left behind."

"She's beautiful!" Violet said, pulling the wriggling little body from the box and cuddling it against her chest.

The dog leaned her head against Nikolai's palm as he reached out to her. "I asked them to give me the most unadoptable dog in the place. The one who had the lowest chance of finding a home. This is who they chose. Apparently, she's been returned a few times. She has some quirks, I guess."

The dog looked kind of like a beagle, but with the scraggly, wiry coat of a terrier. She also had one blue eye, and one brown, which made her gaze oddly piercing as she stared up at Nikolai adoringly.

Yep, Violet decided, quirky would fit into their lives *just* fine.

And Nikolai's choice told her he clearly knew her, how her mind worked, very well. "I love her, Nikolai. But you didn't need to bring presents to convince me to be yours."

He stepped closer. "I didn't?"

"No. Do you remember when I came to find you the morning the police showed up to question you?"

He frowned and she knew he'd likely never forget the day she'd been kidnapped while he was in police custody. "Of course."

She reached out and grabbed his hand. "I was coming to tell you something I've never told anyone before. Not even my parents or my sisters. I really meant it when I said I was yours. Heart, body, soul…it's all yours. I love you, Nikolai. So, so much."

He blinked at her. Then, for a long moment, they just stood there, shocked that their feelings—both their feelings—were finally out in the open.

Feeling like a thousand-pound weight had been lifted from her chest, she smiled up into his confused face and watched as his expression lightened and transformed into a smile that started in his eyes.

Then his expression turned serious again as he turned toward the car and snapped his fingers. "Exhibit B!"

With a long-suffering sigh, Riddick took his time getting out of the car and approaching. When he reached them, he handed Nikolai a small black box and said, "If you ever snap your fingers at me like a dog again, I'll break you in half." Then he was gone.

With a grimace and a muttered curse, Nikolai dropped to his knees in front of her. As he opened the box, he said, "This was my mother's—the only thing of hers I was able to hide and keep when I was sent to the orphanage back in Russia. But if you don't like it, I'll get you whatever you want. Will you marry me, Violet?"

It was a beautiful, cushion-cut, diamond solitaire set in platinum. It was everything she could ever want in a piece of jewelry, but if it came down to it, she'd wear a plastic ring from a gumball machine if Nikolai gave it to her.

Then, a horrible thought occurred to her. "You aren't high on pain meds, are you?"

He laughed. "No. But if you don't say yes or no soon, I'm going to need some."

She set the dog down at her feet, then dropped to her knees in front of Nikolai, staring into his beautiful, warm green eyes. Then she leaned in, kissed him with everything she had, and rested her forehead against his. "Yes. Nothing would make me happier."

He cupped her face and wiped away her tears with his thumbs. "Don't cry, *kotehok*. I can't take it."

"I'm crying because everything is perfect. *You're* perfect."

"Not exactly perfect. I'm pretty sure I can't get up."

Now she was crying and laughing as she helped him to his feet, then snuggled into his chest gently.

Just then, the dog let out a bark that sounded like a witch's cackle. A witch who smoked several packs of cigarettes a day.

"Jesus," she heard Benny mutter. "What the fuck kind of bark was that? Sounds like someone choking a goat."

"Don't blame me. I told him to adopt the Lab mix," Harper said.

Violet glanced down and was greeted with the furious wagging of the dog's little stub tail. Obviously she was protesting not being the center of attention anymore. She scooped her up and kissed her on top of her head. "Quirky, you say?" she teased Nikolai.

He shrugged. "I can handle it if you can."

Violet grinned. "I can handle anything as long as I'm with you."

He bent down and kissed her gently. "Thank God. Because I'm not going anywhere. You believe me, yes?"

She kissed him back. "Of course. I trust you."

"Aw," they heard Harper coo as Seven and Lucas clapped. "Don't you just love a happy ending?"

Violet had never really believed in them before. But now?

"Yes," she murmured against Nikolai's lips. "I do."

The End

But the next book in the series, Semi-Obsessed, is available now on Amazon!

A personal note from Isabel:

If you enjoyed this book, first of all, thanks for reading! It would mean a lot to me if you would take a moment and show your support of indie authors (like me) by leaving a review. Your reviews are a very important part of helping readers discover new books.

Want to know more about me, or when the next book release is? You can email me directly at: isabel.jordan@izzyjo.com. Also feel free to stalk me on:

Bookbub: https://www.bookbub.com/authors/isabel-jordan

Facebook: https://www.facebook.com/AuthorIsabelJordan

Private readers' group (Bitch, write faster): https://www.facebook.com/groups/846416382191567/

Twitter:@izzyjord

Pinterest: https://www.pinterest.com/ijordan0345/

Website: http://www.izzyjo.com/

Sign up for updates on all things Isabel Jordan at: http://www.izzyjo.com/sign-up.html

Thanks so much, and happy reading!

About the author

The normal:

Isabel Jordan writes because it's the only profession that allows her to express her natural sarcasm and not be fired. She is a paranormal and contemporary romance author. Isabel lives in the U.S. with her husband, son, a neurotic Shepherd mix, and a ginormous Great Dane mix named Jerkface. (Don't feel bad for Jerkface. He earned the name.)

The weird:

Now that the normal stuff is out of the way, here's some weird-but-true facts that would never come up in polite conversation. Isabel Jordan:

1. Is terrified of butterflies (don't judge ... it's a real phobia called lepidopterophobia)

2. Is a lover of all things ironic (hence the butterfly on the cover of *Semi-Charmed*)

3. Is obsessed with *Supernatural, Game of Thrones, The Walking Dead,* The 100, Once Upon a Time, and *Dog Whisperer.*

4. Hates coffee. Drinks a Diet Mountain Dew every morning.

5. Will argue to the death that *Pretty in Pink* ended all wrong. (Seriously, she ends up with the guy who was embarrassed to be seen with her and not the nice guy who loved her all along? That would never fly in the world of romance novels.)

6. Would eat Mexican food every day if given the choice.

7. Reads two books a week in varied genres.

8. Refers to her Kindle as "the precious."

9. Thinks puppy breath is one of the best smells in the world.

10. Is a social media idgit. (Her husband had to explain to her what the point of Twitter was. She's still a little fuzzy on what Instagram and Pinterest do.)

11. Kicks ass at Six Degrees of Kevin Bacon.

12. Stole her tagline idea ("weird and proud") from her son. Her tagline idea was, "Never wrong, not quite right." She liked her son's idea better.

13. Breaks one vacuum cleaner a year because she ignores standard maintenance procedures (Really, you're supposed to empty the canister every time you vacuum? Does that seem excessive to anyone else?)

14. Is still mad at the WB network for cancelling *Angel* in 2004.

15. Can't find her way from her bed to her bathroom without her glasses, but refused eye surgery, even when someone else offered to pay. (They lost her at "eye flap". Seriously, look it up. Scary stuff.)

Made in the USA
Las Vegas, NV
22 February 2022